BODY IN THE CANAL

A RITA PATEL MYSTERY

By Catherine Cooper

Oxford eBooks

Chapter

1

"Venice never quite seems real, but rather an ornate film set suspended on the water"

Frida Giannini

Saturday 17th June 2017 2pm

Splash! Priya Shah gasped. She had known this would happen. It had been a mistake to agree to go punting.

Ayeesha had pestered Priya until she agreed to put aside her revision for an afternoon, walk to the Cherwell Boat House and go on the river. It was fine spring weather, and it would be good to get some fresh air and a change of scene, she had conceded. But, really, Priya thought, adjusting the two plaits into which she had tied her brown black hair, as the punt wobbled in the water, going anywhere with Ayeesha was as chaotic as taking a puppy for a walk.

A tall, strong-looking, young woman, Ayeesha had insisted on taking hold of the pole, naturally, and all had gone reasonably well for a while. She had been pretty dextrous, Priya had to admit, standing at the back of the punt. Ayeesha had initially done well, passing the pole through her hands and managing by this means to propel the craft along the shallow water. Then she had become over confident. Borrowing Priya's phone, Ayeesha had attempted to take a video of their excursion, and lost her balance. As she was about to fall, Ayeesha had grabbed on to the pole to steady herself, letting go of Priya's iPhone, which sank heavily to the bottom of the Cherwell river. Great, thought Priya. Everything on the phone was backed up in the Cloud so she wasn't worried about losing data, it was just the inconvenience of being out of touch until she could get a new handset delivered.

"Ooops!" Ayeesha said, "Soz"

Saturday 17th June 2017 2pm

Detective Sergeant Brett McKenzie, standing in a corridor in Leicester Royal Infirmary, sighed at the sound of the voicemail.

"Rita Patel. Student of history and solver of mysteries. Leave a message. If it's interesting I'll call back!"

He gave his name and, stressing the urgency, rang off, hoping for the best. He really needed to speak to Rita.

Saturday 17th June 2017 3pm

Where are you? I sooo need to talk !!! Something random happened. Call me!

Rita Patel emailed her old school friend, Priya Shah. It was a last resort. She had tried messaging and phoning. Where was Priya? Why wasn't she replying? True that, when they last Skyped, Priya had said she would be revising hard for her finals. Her last exams in pre-clinical studies were crucial to her ambitions to be a doctor. But Priya usually had her phone on silent while she studied. Didn't she know Rita needed to talk to her?

Rita paced the floor of the kitchen in her shared student house in Brunswick Street, Leamington Spa, agitated by the thought that she should be revising for her final exams, too. Before she could concentrate, she wanted to talk to Priya! Rita tossed back her long brown curls, and filled the kettle resentfully before switching it on with a sharp flick, as if the appliance had offended her in some way.

Nayan Patel was lounging on the back seat of the number 31 bus, a double decker in loud turquoise. He was on his way from the centre of Leicester to his family home on the south eastern outskirts of the city, in Elm Drive, Oadby. Nayan was returning from a shift as a porter at Leicester Royal Infirmary. This was one of his part-time jobs. Once home he would change, grab some food from the fridge, then set off on his moped to spend a few hours on another job, delivering takeaways.

Nayan, in his first year at De Montfort University, one of two universities in Leicester, was working part-time to finance his studies for a BSc in Psychology and Criminology. He was enjoying it; the course had kicked off with research methods and historical perspectives, and he was taking a module on introduction to criminology. Understanding people was basic to understanding crime, he thought; why people were motivated to act as they did. Criminal profiling, for example, working on the premise that behaviour reflects a person's mental, emotional and personality characteristics, could save hours of detective work. Take the Yorkshire Ripper or the Milly Dowler cases, for instance, where the police forces had been looking for a needle in a hay stack, checking thousands of records relating to vehicles, as that was the only clue they had to go on. An understanding of the kind of person who might commit such a crime could, if used carefully, help to speed up such a search. Technology and profiling were the way forward, he was sure.

Conserving his energy, Nayan lay slumped on the bus, with his long legs curled up against the back of the seat in front. His feet, encased in red Skecher trainers, with the distinctive 'S' logo, were tapping out the rhythm of a rap song beating through his head via the earphones which were lodged in them. Nodding to the beat of the music, Nayan had his eyes closed and was vaguely wondering why the bus was going so slowly. Had he opened his eyes, he would have seen the traffic jam was caused by a build-up of cars on their way to Leicester race course for the Six Hills Handicap. Had he looked up the names of the horses one of them, Glyder, would have caught his attention. But Nayan was in his own world, dreaming of fulfilling his ambition to fly a glider one day soon, it looked so awesome. Rita's friend, Priya, had told him about a gliding centre she had visited with her friend, Ayeesha, at Bicester in Oxfordshire. He had hopes of going on a course at a similar centre nearer his home, in a village called Husbands Bosworth, if he could find the money and the time.

Nayan was almost as tall as his older brother, Mohal, and his face in recent months had thinned to assume similar features to his brother's. Nayan got annoyed when their mother, Padma, sometimes mistook one brother for the other when she was in a hurry, which she often was as she ran a busy dental practice on Uppingham Road, a short drive north from their house if the traffic on the ring road was good. This confusion never happened with his sister, Rita, Nayan thought idly, she was unmistakeable. That reminded him; he had overheard something at the Infirmary that afternoon, just as he was leaving, and needed to tell his brother. The bus finally got to the Oadby racecourse roundabout. Nayan opened his eyes, took up the phone from which he was streaming music, and messaged Mohal.

"Hey bro why are the feds talking to Rita? Tell me what u can!"

Saturday 17th June 2017 3pm

"Bridge" Detective Chief Inspector Jamie Bridge, currently working with the East Midlands Specialist Operations Unit, or EMSOU, sighed as he saw who was calling him on his phone. Typical! He had only dropped into the police headquarters for a short while. He was on his way to a squash game. He wanted quickly to review the statistics for serious and organised crime for a briefing meeting on Monday. He had hoped not to be disturbed.

Jamie Bridge passed a hand over his ginger hair, which he had started to keep close-cropped during his rise in the ranks of the force. In his early thirties, he needed to exude authority and his youthful looks were not advantageous when addressing junior ranks.

"Sorry to bother you, Sir" it was his Sergeant, DS Brett McKenzie "Thought you'd wanna know." Jamie Bridge always found it hard at first to tune in to the Sergeant's New Zealand accent. Despite diversity training, he still had images of rugby games coming into his head when the Sergeant spoke.

"Forensics came up with something odd on the body found in the canal." Perhaps it was not the accent so much as the intonation? the DCI was thinking to himself, while trying to recall the facts of the case. The woman, whose body had been found in the canal at Braunston by magnet fishers, had yet to be identified, he knew. The fishers themselves, shocked to find a dead woman shackled to the shopping trolley which their equipment had locked onto, had seemed genuine to the police officers who attended the scene. It was because the drowning had the hallmarks of gang activity that the discovery had been brought to the attention of his unit.

"Oh?" he asked, distracted, still looking at the crime figures on his computer screen. Violent crime was increasing to a worrying extent. Much of it was drug related. Criminal gangs were moving out of London and the south east- county lines it was called- and bringing a high level of stabbing and shooting incidents with them, often involving very young people. The gangs were hard to stop and operations were hampered by cuts to the service. The blue line was getting very thin indeed, he thought.

Still, they could have it worse. No one could escape the horror of the scenes still coming through from that dreadful fire which had occurred a couple of days ago at Grenfell tower, a block of flats in London. The authorities were being cagey about the number of fatalities, but all the talk among the Chief Inspector's colleagues was that it would be very high. Relatively few people had managed to get out, from what he had seen. The police had their resources stretched, trying to secure the site, helping to identify the deceased, and maintaining public order in the face of considerable, and understandable, anger. At least his team were only looking into one unidentified person, and they had a full body as evidence.

Sergeant McKenzie was talking again. "There was a plastic ID card which had somehow got into the lining of her jacket. We've identified the person it belonged to. It's a female history student at Warwick University." the Sergeant reported, the pitch in his voice going up at the end of his sentences making them seem more like questions than statements. DCI Bridge allowed himself to feel a twinge of hope, maybe this was the breakthrough they needed, he thought, it would be something to tell the Superintendent.

"I managed to speak to her on the phone earlier today. She mentioned your name?" the Sergeant continued.

"Oh?" this time the officer had Jamie Bridge's attention. He stopped looking at the crime figures.

"The name on the ID was Rita Patel." the Sergeant waited for his boss to respond.

Detective Chief Inspector Jamie Bridge hit his forehead with his hand and groaned. It was going to be a long afternoon after all. He had better cancel the squash court.

Saturday 17th June 2017 4pm

Unable to concentrate on her studies, Rita had taken a bus

and was walking through the centre of Warwick, trying to calm her nerves over the call she was expecting. Priya had still not got back to her and there was no one else she wanted to confide in. Most of her time studying at Warwick University was spent on the campus, which was nearer to Coventry than anywhere else. Sometimes, for a change, she liked to catch the uni bus to the town of Warwick itself, to take in the history. There was the castle of course, which everyone knew about, and the timber-framed Lord Leycester Hospital, which went back to the 14th century, but there were other old buildings she liked to pass as she walked along. It would refresh her mind for further revision, she told herself.

She had grabbed her turquoise hoody as she left the shared house and now put her hands in its pockets. Under the hoody she wore a white T-shirt and black joggers, her Office ankle boots completing the outfit. She had applied minimal make up to her face, a face which she rued every time she looked in the mirror. Why had she inherited her mother's round features and snub nose? Her curly brown hair she had fastened against her head with a large silver clip. A black triangular- shaped day pack was fastened against the front of her body. There had been a spate of bag thefts by boys on bikes near the campus, so she had learnt to take no chances. The word was that the university was looking into paying the police to patrol the area. Rita was glad she would be leaving uni soon and would no longer have to worry about being mugged there.

Rita had reached St Mary's church in the centre of Warwick when the phone in her pocket started to vibrate. She hoped it was Priya at last. She swiped the screen with her thumb to answer.

"Rita" a familiar voice said, a voice she had not heard in a long while.

"You and I need to chat" DCI Jamie Bridge added.

Rita leaned against the side of the medieval church

building, comforted by the history which she knew lay inside. The church was closed to visitors now, of course, but she had often visited the magnificent collection of tombs in the Beauchamp chapel. She listened as the Chief Inspector spoke.

"My Sergeant called you earlier." he said, "As he told you, we need to identify a woman. She had something belonging to you in her coat. I want to describe her to you. See if you can tell us who she is."

"Oh?" Rita had thought this was going to be an odd business. Sergeant McKenzie had been evasive on the phone earlier when she had replied to his voicemail message and asked him what this was about, "Can't you send a picture to my phone?" she asked the Chief Inspector.

"No" the DCI said shortly, familiar with Rita's curiosity, "Just listen."

"All right" Rita said reluctantly, wondering what was coming.

Chapter

2

"Everything in Venice is just a little bit creepy, as much as it's beautiful."

Christopher Moore

Saturday 17th June 2017 5pm

The sky was clouding over and drizzle was threatening. Rita, still propped up against an ancient buttress of the church in the centre of Warwick, pulled her hood over her head and hunched her shoulders. She could have found somewhere warmer and dryer inside, but this wasn't a conversation she wanted to have indoors where she might be overheard.

Detective Chief Inspector Bridge was painting a picture of a woman in her mid- thirties or thereabouts with shoulder length brown hair; she was a little taller than Rita, just over 170 centimetres, compared to her 167, apparently, and had been wearing a light blue waterproof jacket – "Berghaus if that makes any difference" – a grey T- shirt, and dark blue convertible walking trousers – "I gather that means you can wear them short or long, if you see what I mean. She had quite large eyes in relation to her face and a brown mole on her left cheek" DCI Bridge completed his summary.

Light dawned in Rita's mind. "OMG!" she exclaimed loudly to the alarm of a teenage dog walker passing by. "I can't be sure, but it sounds like a woman …." she had paused for a moment, seeking the right words, "I met when I was in Venice." she finally finished her sentence.

"Mmmnh" Jamie Bridge seemed to be taking this in. "Do you have a name by any chance?" he asked hopefully.

"Olga Kelenko. That's the name she gave me. She was

brought here from the Ukraine by her mother." Rita told him, "That was when she was young. She took British citizenship and is working here, in the UK I mean. Why are you interested in her?" Rita wanted to know.

"That's really helpful, Rita." the DCI said, and then checked the spelling of the name with her but gave nothing away. "We may need to talk to you further. I'm afraid to tell you that she's been found dead, in Leicestershire. Actually, it was in the canal at Braunston, just before the tunnel, you may know the place?"

Rita nodded, not speaking. She was absorbing the shock that this person had died, and clearly in suspicious circumstances, since the police were speaking to her. She was also trying to take in the fact that she had been found in a spot local to, and known to, Rita. What was Olga doing there? she wondered.

Rita could picture the tunnel on the canal at Braunston, they had been through it on a barge holiday as children, her father thinking they should know more about the heritage of Leicestershire, their county. Perhaps her father was where she had got her interest in history from, she thought. The waterway, the Leicester Line as it was called, had originally been two canals, which were bought out by the Grand Junction Canal Company in the 1840s. Linking up with the navigable part of the River Soar, the canals ran south from Braunston to London, with arms reaching out to Market Harborough and Welford. The waterway had once been important for industry, providing the East Midlands coalfields with direct access to the capital. Now, like the holiday that Rita and her family had enjoyed, the canal was used for leisure, Foxton Locks, with its staircase of locks, being a particularly picturesque and popular spot for day trips. Rita could picture the entrance to the tunnel at Braunston where Olga had been found. Grassy banks came down to the canal at that point. Was that how Olga had got there, or had she gone into the water from a boat? Rita was not sure how much the police would tell her.

"Can I Skype you after the weekend? You can ask me anything else you need to know from me then?" Rita asked. "I am in the middle of my final exams." she told the Chief Inspector, "I can call you on Monday afternoon when I have finished another paper. But I won't be free to come to Leicester, if that's what you need, until later next week".

"I suppose Skype will have to do" Jamie Bridge sighed, shaking his head when he noticed the time on his computer screen which was still trying to show him the crime figures. He passed a hand through his ginger hair again. He would be bald soon, he could feel it; dealing with Rita Patel was never straightforward, he thought.

* * *

Ending the call, Rita headed into a Caffe Nero not far from the church and bought a mug of mint tea and her favourite wafer biscuits to consume while she settled her nerves. The call from DCI Bridge had sparked memories. Rita put her phone back in her pocket and, staring out of the window at the quiet streets of Warwick, populated at this time of day by shoppers and shop workers going home, plus a few homeless people begging for change or looking for doorways in which to bed down later, she thought back to when she met Olga Kelenko.

* * *

Venice was where she had spent her first term of this, her final, academic year, on a study course arranged by the History Department. Travelling on her own from Birmingham to Marco Polo Airport, late in September, Rita was one of the last students to arrive from Warwick. She had caught a water bus, as suggested in the notes she had been sent by the university. On the crossing to Venice, Rita had tried to take a few pictures with her phone, but was jolted about as the craft hurtled across the expanse of water and bounced her up and down in an alarming manner, only slowing as it approached the narrow canals of the city itself and sought its berth. For someone from Leicester, where traffic on the canals moved sedately, this was very disconcerting.

Rita had disembarked shakily and consulted her phone for directions to the room provided by her host family, noticing how crowded were the waterside walks and bridges which linked the different parts of the city. This was not going to be easy, she thought.

"Scusa?" "Mi puo aiutare?" With her backpack hoisted behind her and her light blue suitcase wheeled alongside like an obedient dog, Rita had felt very awkward as she tried to follow her route. She managed to negotiate a narrow bridge and then some uneven steps, squeezing between rows of people who came towards her in waves, impeding her progress. "Scusa. Scusa." she repeated as she went. The building she needed was not far away now, through an alleyway to her left and then across a square. Once her destination was in sight, she allowed herself to breathe deeply. Rita staggered to the side door as instructed and rang the bell.

Rita found she had been given a small room on the top floor of an apartment which was above a busy trattoria. The apartment belonged to the family who ran the restaurant. From her roof top location Rita had a bird's eye view of the small square below, the orange and white awning of the trattoria stretching across a corner of the busy thoroughfare. The orange chairs of the café spread towards the middle of the square during the day and were stacked in piles at the edge at the end of each evening. If she looked really hard, through a gap in the buildings opposite she could see a glint of silver which was the canal. That must be the alley way through which she had walked when she arrived, she thought, trying to get her bearings.

Her lectures, she learnt at the orientation meeting the next day, were scheduled for 9am most mornings, allowing time for visits to galleries and other research in the afternoons. The trattoria, she found, barely rested between late night carousing and morning breakfasting, so that in the early weeks, until she had got used to her work pattern and to the noise below her, Rita had been very short of sleep. Thinking back to her time in Venice, as she finished her tea in Caffe Nero, Rita thought this might be one reason why she had failed to notice, at first, that Olga Kelenko was following her.

Saturday 17th June 2017 8pm

"So, you did know her?" Priya was talking to Rita at last. When Priya had told her friend about how her phone ended up in the river, Rita had commiserated and agreed that Ayeesha was not the most reliable person to go punting with.

"I nearly had a heart attack!" Priya had told her friend, "I could see someone, or something, was going in the water!"

"Choose a better companion next time" Rita had advised, thinking of the skill of the gondoliers she had seen when she was in Venice.

The Venetians, she had learnt, had settled in that inhospitable water-laden area, where malaria was a constant risk, for a reason. They were escaping from the ravages of the Huns over 1500 years ago. An adaptable people, they had learned how to drive wooden piles into the water to enable them to build. They had created the canals along the sides of which they had erected their houses and palaces, and they had developed over the centuries from fishermen, to traders, to merchant princes, amassing great wealth by trade and other less legal means. The shallow water on which the current city was built had protected them from attack as no fleet could enter it, but the very water that protected them was also a threat to their existence as it eroded the buildings and there was frequent flooding. The locals, she had seen, were water creatures, skilled in various types of boats. The gondoliers had been very demonstrative, but they knew what they were doing. They were not above knocking into other craft to make their way through the busy waterways.

Priya had not been too surprised to hear about Rita's calls from the police. These things were always happening to Rita, she thought, hoping her friend had not got herself into deep water.

"Did I know her, Olga Kelenko, well, not exactly, I mean it was like…." Now that she could talk about it, Rita found it hard to find the words.

Priya sensed trouble. "Oh, Rita what now? What have you got yourself into?" Priya, in her Merton College room, kicked off the sandals she had changed into after their escapades on the river. She had also shed the dungarees and top in favour of a roomy yellow shirt and black leggings. She was talking to Rita on Facetime, resting her iPad against the cushions on her bed so she could stretch out next to it after a rather stressful day relaxing with Ayeesha.

Rita, she could see, was sitting at her lap top which was on the desk in her room in the house she shared with Sammi and her other student friends. Priya wondered if Rita had added any more stickers to her lap top cover, she was always picking them up at talks and demonstrations. As Rita spoke, Priya settled on her back, her head propped up on another of the colourful cushions she had purchased from the covered market in Oxford. One of her legs was stretched out, the other bent at the knee. Priya laid one hand near the iPad, while the other was stroking her long, straight brown black hair, which she wore loose, as she gazed at her friend's face.

"Yeh, yeh, I met her" Rita was saying. "It was pretty scary, actually. She was, like, following me, you know."

Priya sat upright quickly, startled. "We should talk about this," she urged, sitting up and settling her back against the head rest of the bed and the tablet on her lap so she could concentrate, her left hand stroking her hair more vigorously, "Tell me everything!"

* * *

It had been a strange time. As well as the work and the constant noise at the trattoria, there was the language and the geography of the City to adjust to, all of which made it hard for Rita to think straight, she realised, looking back. The weather had affected her badly, too. At first it was warmer than she had expected, and very humid, creating a heavy atmosphere. The temperature soon changed while she there, falling from around 20 degrees at the beginning, when she could wear T-shirts during the day, to about 10 degrees in November, and falling further by the time her course finished in December, hardly reaching much above zero during the day and going below freezing at night, by which time there were some flurries of snow in the cold wind and she was wearing a couple of jumpers and her quilted jacket. No matter what the temperature, the high humidity persisted, something she only gradually grew used to. Every day was like walking into a shower room or a laundrette, she thought. Rita supposed it was the proximity of the water that had this effect. Not only did it make her brain feel a bit foggy but actual fog rolled in during the late autumn. Clouds of grey hung over the waterways, which some of her friends on the course said made the place feel magical, but, for Rita, the fog only added to a general feeling she had while in Venice of disorientation.

The autumn of 2016 had been a weird time to be British and studying abroad, everyone agreed. The EU referendum vote was fresh in people's minds and it was creating uncertainty in the minds of the students and their tutors. What should their futures be? Where should they seek to settle? Would there even be a repeat of this part of the course, which had run for many years? Or would they be the last to take part in it? Sometimes, local people, or foreign visitors to Venice, would look at the English students with sympathy in their eyes and say something like "so sorry you are leaving us".

Fortunately, no one was seriously hostile, unlike the debates in her own country which had become very animated as the day of the referendum drew nearer, culminating in that dreadful shooting of the MP Jo Cox. There were other less traumatic but still unedifying episodes – the clash of boats on the Thames between Bob Geldoff and Nigel Farage being one, the Leave campaign bus claiming that £350,000 could be diverted from the EU to the NHS being another. In the end, by a narrow margin, the emotional appeal of the Leave side, combined with the charisma of Boris Johnson and unpleasant insinuations from the UKIP party about migrants from Turkey, had succeeded where the forecasts of 'experts' about the effects of leaving the EU on the UK economy had failed.

Whatever the reasons for the vote, the result of the referendum had been like an earthquake, with tremors and aftershocks reverberating, and the political parties divided and at odds about what should happen next. Emotions were running high and sensible debate seemed to have gone out of the window. David Cameron had left the stage promptly and Theresa May, the new Prime Minister, in default of any other contenders, was to be seen meeting and greeting European leaders, in a way that looked rather unnatural and uncomfortable for her, Rita felt, in an effort to negotiate a Brexit deal.

It was in this unreal atmosphere, at home and abroad, that Rita tried to get grips with her studies and with living abroad, and to navigate her way around a strange city. She found Venice slightly claustrophobic, with its small squares and tall buildings, hemmed in by the canals. St Mark's Square was one of the few large spaces, and she could understand why the Venetians had created it. This large square, surrounded by famous buildings, many of the statues and much of the decoration for which had been plundered from Constantinople during and after the 4th Crusade, had witnessed civic gatherings for over 800 years. It was standing in the square, looking at the magnificent Basilica with all its rich ornamentation, and reading about how the body of St Mark had been stolen from Alexandria in the 9th century to boost the reputation of Venice, that Rita had first noticed the woman.

This was about three weeks into her course. She saw her several times more until she almost expected to come across her in the city at some point in the day, Rita confided to Priya.

"I was, like, surely it's a coincidence? Or, am I going nuts, maybe there are lots of women who look like that?" Rita said.

After all, there had been nothing distinctive about her, really. She was a bit taller than Rita perhaps -not difficult her brothers would say- and 10 years older, maybe more? Rita hadn't wanted to stare, so she only caught snatches of the woman and couldn't form a whole picture. But, after she had spotted her a few times, it seemed to Rita that this was more than accidental.

"I was like, hey, what's going on?" Rita told Priya.

"Didn't you tell anyone?" Priya asked.

"No, no, no." Rita shook her head. "I didn't know anyone well enough to mention it. The others on the course would've thought I'd lost it!"

But Rita had been concerned. There were so many people in Venice moving around all the time. Why would she keep seeing this one? There were lots of tourists crowding together in the popular areas, like the market and bridge at the Rialto. The visitors were of every nationality, often in groups identifiable by colourful back packs, or scarves, or by a leader holder aloft a furled umbrella, or a small flag. They were difficult to pass on the bridges and in narrow passageways. Other tourists wandered in twos or threes, often stopping at the most inconvenient places to check maps, or their phones, or to take selfies against the backdrop of the jewel-like buildings. Threading their way between the tourists were those locals who were left – their numbers were diminishing every year, Rita had read.

Some residents disliked the visitors, Rita had learnt from the gossip at the trattoria. They felt the city was being turned into a sort of Disneyland for foreigners instead of being a vibrant place where people lived and worked. Especially resented were the large cruise ships which passed through St Marks Basin, their bland white sides looming over the ancient delicate architecture, and the wash they create threatening to bring down the very sights they were trying to see.

With the main bridges and routes so crowded, Rita quickly learnt better ways to get through the maze to her lectures and to the sights she wanted to visit, where this was possible. This was when she realised that the woman must be following her, there was no other explanation. Sometimes she saw her as she walked to her morning lecture, warm ciabatta bread, which the family had given her, in her hand. Once it was when she was with a group of friends from the course, tucking into pasta in a bar. Then there was that time in one of the many churches which they visited as part of their studies.

Exasperated, one day Rita had decided to see if there was any way of shaking the woman off, she told Priya, to test the theory that she was being followed. One afternoon, when the lectures had finished and she should have been in the library, Rita had set off to carry out her plan. She walked to St Mark's Square. Scanning the entrances and exits between the Basilica, the Doge's Palace, the Campanile, or bell tower, and the Clock Tower, she spotted the woman pretending to examine a stand of postcards. Rita criss-crossed the square to keep her guessing about where she was headed next and, noting for future reference the police post-marked "Polizia"- on one side of the square, took an exit near it.

The arcade which she entered was lined with shops and cafes and led to a small square bathed in shadow. From there she took another random exit and kept turning right and then left until she wound her way to another canal where she could catch a vaporetto. Rita got off after two stops, leaving it until the last minute and stepping off confidently as she had seen the locals do. After that, she dawdled in a tourist shop, and then dashed into a church she had visited before, entering by one door and leaving quickly by another. Emotionally and physically tired by now, and haunted by the idea of the woman's presence, Rita had reached the Galleria Dell Academia before she allowed herself to look round. The woman wasn't there!

Rita, feeling pleased with herself, had taken a vaporetto back to the trattoria above which she was living. Wearily, she had climbed the three flights of stairs, her pink satchel bag swinging heavily on her right shoulder, her blue jacket clutched in her left hand as all the activity had made her feel rather warm. Rita was looking forward to a long cold glass of water in her room. She had left the shutters closed when she went out so she switched on the light as soon as she entered, shaking off her shoes and enjoying the feel of the tiled floor on her tired feet as she walked barefoot to get the bottle of water out of the small fridge with which the room was provided. She put her bag and jacket on the wicker chair which was placed between the bed and the window.

Having gulped down some of the water, Rita had shaken her head at her foolishness. She must have been wrong about this woman, she thought. Perhaps being in a foreign country had made her paranoid. Thinking it was time to let in some natural light, Rita stood at the window and opened the shutters. She gazed down from her eyrie onto the square below. The orange chairs of the trattoria, arranged neatly in rows at the start of the day, were now scattered haphazardly around like guests towards the end of a party. Beyond the chairs, at the opposite side of the square, to one side of the entrance to the alley way which led to the canal, were a few lemon trees, offering welcome shade when the weather was hot, and, as Rita looked out, casting shadows across the square in the evening light. Standing in those shadows, and looking up at the flat, was the unmistakable figure of the woman who had been following Rita.

Chapter

3

"When I seek another word for 'music', I never find any other word than 'Venice'."

Friedrich Nietzsche

Saturday 17th June 2017 8.30pm

"Oh no!" Priya gasped. "You hadn't got rid of her at all?"

"No" Rita sighed, "And what was even worse was that she knew where I lived. So, all my efforts to shake her off were wasted. She just had to wait 'til I got back."

"That must have been very worrying" Priya spoke sympathetically, "Did you report her to the authorities then?"

"Well, no." Rita conceded.

Typical! Priya thought, lifting her eyes to the ceiling. Rita would think she could handle the situation herself.

"Well, first, what exactly would I say? And, second, my Italian wasn't up to 'I think a woman is following me'. It didn't come up in the vocab I studied." Rita protested.

"OK" Priya conceded, not really sure her friend's excuses held up. "So how did you find out who she was?"

"Well, it blew me away for a bit, to be honest," Rita confessed to her friend. "I had some more water while I thought about it, and I hatched a plan."

Oh no, thought Priya, what was coming next? It sounded like it was going to be a long story.

"Shall we take a break?" Priya offered. "I totally want to carry on but I'm busting for the loo."

"Yeh. See you in five." Rita agreed and they signed off temporarily.

"Talking to Rita?" Ayeesha put her head round the door of Priya's room just as she was emerging from her en suite bathroom, a luxury for which she was grateful after the bathing facilities in the student house they had shared together in Howard Street. Having Ayeesha in the room next to her meant there was still little privacy, however, unless Priya chose to lock her out, which she was loathe to do, it seemed so unfriendly. Priya and a couple of friends had found a flat in Headington, another area of Oxford and near the hospital, to share the next year, assuming they would be continuing with their medical studies. Priya was starting to wonder how much privacy she would get there.

"How did you guess?" Priya asked, brushing at her iPad to continue the conversation with her old school friend.

"I could tell by the sound of your voice" Ayeesha laughed. "Is she involved in one of her investigations again?"

"I do hope not." Priya said earnestly, "She's got finals like us, she can't afford to get tied up with any more mysteries. But you know what Rita's like! "

Ayeesha nodded in understanding, swinging her legs alternately as she continued to stand in the doorway.

"Sorry if I was disturbing you, by the way, these walls are rather thin." Priya added, hoping Ayeesha would take the hint and leave.

"It's cool." Ayeesha shrugged her shoulders "Give her my best wishes" and, finally, she turned and bounded out in her usual energetic fashion.

Rita was already calling in. Priya accepted and the two friends could see each other again. Priya, perched at her own desk now, saw Rita was still sitting on a red wooden chair in her room in the house in Leamington Spa. When she had first moved in with Daz and the others, Rita had treated Priya to a video tour, providing a commentary as she 'took' her friend from room to room, Rita providing a commentary. It was an end of terrace late Victorian house, which had been adapted to fit 6 student bedrooms, as well as a communal kitchen, and Priya saw behind every door, courtesy of Rita's phone. Rita had told Priya she had felt at home there from the moment she crossed the doorway at the suggestion of her friend, Sammi. Hers was the small room to the left at the top of the stairs, with the tall narrow window at the front of the house. In her tenure of over two years, she had had chances to swap for a larger room at the back of the house, overlooking the garden, but she preferred to have a view of the street, just like the one she had in her old room at home, before she had given it up to Nayan.

Sammi, as the oldest of their group, occupied the downstairs room next to the hall and with a bay window jutting out next to the green front door. In the bay Sammi had placed a large sofa and some bean bags, so, as Priya had seen from pictures posted by her friend, it had become a place for the housemates to gather for a catch- up from time to time, the kitchen being adequate for cooking purposes but not large enough for them all to hang out. The front garden, which Rita had included in the video tour, was covered in practical but attractive grey slate chippings alongside the tarmacked path where they kept the inevitable bins bulging with the discarded contents of the house. Priya recalled it had been the same with their shared house in Howard Street; house fronts were for bikes and bins, and sometimes a traffic cone or a shopping trolley if one had found its way home after a particularly good night out. Rita had shown her friend the back garden, after walking through the kitchen with a cursory shot of the work surfaces which were almost completely covered in bottles of soft drinks, cereal boxes and bags of pasta. The garden was an expanse of timber strips, resembling a ship's deck. There were a couple of benches to sit on, should the weather be fine enough, and, judging by the detritus around them, used by those who smoked. As usual, any kind of smoking indoors, including vaping, was in breach of the tenancy agreement.

When she heard that Priya was moving to a college room for her last year, Rita had shaken her head and said it was not for her. She said her housemates had been so supportive after all that business when she got kidnapped that Rita didn't want to leave them for the sake of moving to university accommodation for her last year. They were all happy to go on sharing together. It worked very well. Sammi had a car he kept in Leamington and did any heavy shopping that they forgot to order on-line, some of the others took it in turns to cook supper and Rita's job was to keep the shared areas clean and tidy.

"How's that going, sis?" her brother, Mohal, had laughed when he heard. Rita was not renowned for her domestic skills.

"OK thanks." she told him, thinking back to the mess he and his friends had left behind during his student days at Hertfordshire uni. All her housemates were reasonably tidy, so the cleaning did not take too long. Every time it came to wiping down the bathroom, though, Rita would think back to her encounter with the woman who been following her in Venice and she would wonder how she had the nerve to confront her. She shuddered to think what might have happened.

"So, did you meet her then?" Priya prompted, "The woman they've found in the canal at Braunston?"

"Oh yes." Rita confirmed, nodding. Rita was looking tired Priya thought. This extra strain, brought on by contact with the police, was not good on top of her final exams. Her curly hair was escaping from the knot on top of her head and tumbling around her ears, her baggy turquoise T-shirt looked creased and slightly stained. Was Rita looking after herself? Priya wondered. She had placed her own sandals back in the shoe rack she kept by her wardrobe. Rita's brown flats could, by contrast, be seen marooned on their sides on the blue rug in her room, like two small shipwrecks.

"I decided to trap her" Rita told her friend.

Priya swallowed, "What did you do?" she asked, after she had sighed disapprovingly.

"I went about as normal for a couple of days." Rita said. "And I noticed her now and again."

"Weren't you frightened?" Priya asked.

"I just wanted to know what was going on." Rita told her "And I had a lot to think about, what with my work, and Matteo…"

Oh yes, Priya thought, I wondered when we would get to him, the famous Matteo, who Rita had met on her first day in Italy, the son of the family at the trattoria, who sometimes waited on tables there. Matteo, who Rita had been seeing for a few months both during and after her Venice study trip. Matteo, who pulled Rita away from seeing Priya in favour of visits to Venice, such as for the Carnival in February. It was fair to say that Rita had been pretty distracted. Then, during the Easter break from uni, just when hysteria about their finals was beginning to kick in, Matteo had ended their relationship and the Venice trips suddenly stopped.

Rita had taken the break-up pretty well, Priya had thought, especially given the crap timing. Rita's previous relationship, with her actor boyfriend, Jacob, had ended amicably not long before she went to Venice, Priya recalled. Jacob had been offered a role in a forthcoming drama being commissioned by a US cable network and filmed in Durham, in the North East of England. It would be intense, he had told Rita, and it wouldn't be fair to try to continue to see each other. Priya thought he still messaged Rita occasionally, and kept her up to date with the dramas off the set as well as on. Matteo, by contrast, had given no reason for the break-up that Priya knew of; far from keeping in touch, he had ghosted her friend, ceasing all contact and ignoring Rita's messages. He had behaved very badly, and Priya thought any resentment she felt towards him was justified on her friend's behalf.

"So, the third day I left the flat and made sure she was following me." Rita resumed her story about how she came to meet Olga Kelenko.

"You made sure?" Priya asked.

"Yeh. I went slow and gave her every chance to catch up." Rita confirmed.

"The opposite to what you did before?" Priya checked.

"Yes, but I didn't let on that I knew she was there. It was fun really." Rita smiled. Priya thought it didn't sound like fun and shook her head, her hair swishing like a bead curtain and then falling back into place gracefully.

"Sometimes when I did look for her, she would have changed her appearance – a different scarf, for example, or she might carry her jacket over her arm. But I always knew it was her."

"Describe her then." Priya was keen to know more.

"Oh, I'll get to that." Rita said enigmatically, wanting to keep to her way of telling her story.

"Eventually I came to Santa Croce, which is one of the quieter areas of the city, and I went into a trattoria on the square, the Campo San Giacomo d'ell Orio."

Priya smiled at the way the Venetian place names rolled off Rita's tongue. It had not been like that when she first started to learn Italian, she remembered.

"I walked to the ladies' loo." Rita was saying, "It was a place I knew from a previous visit. Proper facilities, not those footprint loos which tourists find so horrifying at some of the well-known tourist places, like the opera at Verona." Rita told Priya.

"Really? They still have those?" Priya's hand went to her mouth in horror. She had seen some primitive arrangements on visits to India, when they had toured a number of rural villages connected with her father's family in times past, but it seemed strange to her that prosperous European countries would continue these traditions.

"Oh yes. Some people on the course went there and were most surprised. They said the locals just shrugged and said it was normal." Rita explained.

"Even so…" Priya began.

"But that's not the point." Rita interrupted, eager to get away from a discussion of public toilet facilities and back to her tale.

Rita had been waiting in a cubicle for about five minutes, hoping no other customers would come in and disturb her plan, she told her friend. Just as she thought she could not wait any longer, the door to the ladies squeaked open, and under the door of her cubicle Rita could see feet encased in grey hiking boots beneath brown walking trousers. The feet went into the cubicle next to hers. Rita had then exited and stood by the sink, pretending to wash her hands but all the while checking in the mirror in front of her. As she expected, the cubicle's occupant came out and Rita got a good look at her reflection before she whipped round to face her.

"Why are you following me?" she had snapped fiercely as the woman stepped back in alarm.

Chapter

4

"There is something so different in Venice from any other place in the world, that you leave at once all accustomed habits and everyday sights to enter an enchanted garden"

Mary Shelley

Friday 14th October 2016 4pm

"Perche stai facendo questo?" Rita added in her best Italian accent, her arms outstretched in exasperation, then she repeated herself, this time in English, because it felt more natural "Why are you doing this?"

The woman's reply left Rita with her mouth hanging open. She said, in English, "Sorry, Rita. You weren't supposed to notice. But I guess I'm not very good at this."

"You'd better explain." Rita said firmly, feeling surprisingly angry now she was face to face with her stalker who, she found, knew her name. Rita was pressing her hands behind her against the cool of the white hand basin, ready to launch herself towards the door if things got difficult. The woman might be slightly taller than her but she didn't look particularly fit. Rita thought she could take her in a fight if she needed to; but she really didn't want to do that.

"Let's get a cup of tea." said the woman.

In the event, they both ordered an iced lemonade and a pistachio pastry, specialities of the trattoria, at the counter. They found seats in a booth in a corner and sat confronting one another. Rita had taken the place facing the door. She had read about such things. This seat gave her maximum opportunity to observe the room, who came in and who went out, as well as good access to the door if she needed to leave urgently. What if the woman had an accomplice, for example, who might come in at any moment? After her kidnapping episode, Rita was not going to take any unnecessary risks.

"I'm sorry if I frightened you." the woman said.

"Not at all." Rita shook her head of curly hair in defiance, not wanting to admit the thoughts that had been going through her head.

"My name is Olga Kelenko," the woman was staring at Rita with large blue eyes. She turned to search in the capacious light blue bag she had been carrying on her shoulder. The bag looked like it would fold up small if needed. It matched her jacket Rita noticed. With her brown walking trousers, she would fit in well with the tourists in the city she thought. It was only because Rita was curious that she had spotted her. What was she looking for, Rita wondered? Not a weapon surely?

The woman she now knew as Olga took out a business card and gave it to her. It was printed in a standard format by one of those firms which advertise on daytime TV, but the phone number had been blacked out in pen and rewritten in a neat hand.

"And?" Rita said, taking the card reluctantly. She was no wiser.

"I've lived in the UK since I was small. My parents brought me there from Ukraine. I used to be a teacher" Olga said, irrelevantly as far as Rita could see, "but there was an incident, well it wasn't an incident really…" She spoke very well, Rita thought, but was there a hint of an Eastern European accent? Or was she imagining it now she knew the woman was Olga from the Ukraine?

"Do I need to know this?" Rita butted in. It was rude of her, she knew, but Olga's autobiography would not explain her presence – in this trattoria, on this day, on the trail of Rita.

"Well, anyway," Olga continued, "There were allegations, but nothing was proved, because nothing happened," she put the emphasis on 'nothing' when she used the word, "but mud sticks doesn't it, it was recorded on what was then my CRB record, you see, even though the police didn't pursue it…"

"And?" Rita said, abruptly, folding her arms. Now she was thinking this woman might be crazy. Was she one of those obsessed stalkers who won't go away?

"I just wanted you to know that I'm not dangerous. I've never hurt anyone. I don't think I could, even if someone attacked me." Olga had waved her hands around as she spoke, threatening to knock her pastry to the floor.

Rita could picture their interview, in the corner of the red and white trattoria. Those precise words came back to her as she told her story to Priya, settled at her desk in the student house. Someone had attacked Olga it seemed. Someone had made sure she ended up in the canal near Leicester. Why? Olga had not said she had any connection with the city as far as Rita could remember. She wished now she had paid more attention, but she was too annoyed at the time.

"There wasn't much else I could do besides teaching," Olga had gone on with her life story, her accent getting more pronounced, Rita thought. It gave Rita a chance to check out her appearance properly across the red plastic table, while Rita made sure her own face continued to wear an expression of exasperation. Olga had shoulder length brown hair cut in a tidy bob, a faint brown mole on her left cheek, and large eyes that opened like flowers when she was excited; those were the features Rita recalled. Although the other woman was a little taller than Rita when they were standing up, sitting down their eyes were level. Rita noticed that Olga had a slight build. Her shoulders were probably narrower than Rita's. She had been right about being able to take her on physically. But that looked like it was not going to be necessary.

"My IT skills aren't great but I am very observant, like

yourself." she flicked Rita a sly look from under her eye lashes as she paid her quarry this compliment. So, she knew that I knew she was following me, Rita thought.

Rita shook her head questioningly. What was the point of this? The ice in their drinks was melting, her sticky pastry was a distant memory, and still Rita had no idea why she had been followed.

"There weren't many openings for people like me. I decided to start my own business, as a claims investigator. I work for insurance companies mostly but I've also done surveillance for DWP – the Department for Work and Pensions- they have a fraud section for when people claim benefits and the Department thinks they might be lying about their circumstances or health condition. People on disability benefits who ride horses or regularly referee football matches, or people not being truthful about their relationship status, that sort of thing."

Rita nodded. Olga was a private investigator; well that made sense of a sort, she supposed.

Saturday 17th June 2017 9pm

"A detective!" Priya broke in on the story, sitting forward excitedly. "Who was she acting for?"

"If you'll let me continue, I'll tell you" Rita answered, a little huffily, having had her flow interrupted again.

"She was working for an investment bank." Rita told her surprised friend.

Rita continued, explaining what Olga had divulged as they swilled the last pieces of ice in their glasses and finished their lemonades. "Apparently the bank had recently put money into a hotel and restaurant chain with branches all over Europe. The due diligence - that's the checks they do before they invest - had not given them any cause for concern, but the financial figures they were now receiving as shareholders showed amounts of money passing through some of the businesses which could not be explained by normal customer numbers. Something else was going on."

Sunday 18th June 2017 3am

"So, what was she like?" Given the hour, Priya and Rita were talking quietly iPad screen to iPad screen, lying in their beds.

During their earlier conversation, Rita's phone had unexpectedly started to play 'City of Stars', her latest ringtone; she had been enthralled by the film La La Land. It was her mother, Padma. Rita had apologised to Priya – "She's only calling to nag me about getting enough sleep and eating fruit and veg." Rita had said. "And she usually tells me about next door's cat!" she had laughed as she signed off with Priya and answered the call.

"Oh Rita", her mother began, "I am glad you answered, I wanted to see how you are, how the exams are going?"

"Everything's fine, Mum" Rita replied, quickly deciding not to mention the call from the police, her mother would only worry.

"Not working too hard, eh?" her mother checked, "You are making sure you get to bed early? You need your sleep."

"Yes Mum," Rita spoke with her fingers crossed so it didn't count as a lie.

"And you are eating well? Lots of fruit and vegetables to keep up your vitamin C? Only I can send you some samosas if you would like." Padma pressed. "It's OK Mum," Rita said, "There are samosas in Leamington. Not as good as yours of course."

"And you are not getting into any trouble?" Padma probed, "It's just that Nayan heard a policeman on the telephone at the Infirmary and he thought he heard your name mentioned."

"Oh no," Rita still had her fingers crossed, "Nothing to worry about. How's next door's cat doing, by the way?" Rita had changed the subject swiftly.

∗ ∗ ∗

It was now three in the morning. Padma would not approve, Rita thought, but neither young woman could sleep so they might as well talk, as long as they did not wake their neighbours. "I'll get up at 10" Rita promised herself. Her next exam was on Monday in the afternoon and she had done most of the revision, it was just a case of refreshing her mind on the main points.

"Like you might expect a teacher to be." Rita answered Priya's question about Olga Kelenko's appearance, "That's what she told me, that she had been a teacher but lost her job over a misunderstanding or something, and started investigating insurance claims. It sounded interesting work. She had moved on from benefit fraud and matrimonial cases and was looking into claims under international contracts. The sort of thing where the goods were alleged to have been stolen en route or lost in an accident. Some of them turned out to be fake, of course. It was her job to find out which ones." Rita explained some more.

"Mmmn. That sort of work would be interesting for you." Priya observed. She was lying on her stomach, her tablet sitting on the cushions at the top of the bed, her long brown black hair untied and falling evenly on either side of her head. Rita should be a detective, she had always liked to solve mysteries, she thought.

"She was kind of not noticeable" Rita went on unhelpfully "Useful for a detective I s'pose. Mid-thirties, a bit taller than me, brown hair. She had a roundish face with large eyes that could suddenly look at you sharply. She had a brown mole on her cheek but it wasn't that noticeable when she was talking to you. She wore clothes like a tourist would wear, so she could blend in. She had studied Classics and taught

Philosophy, Religion and Ethics. I guess there's no demand in schools for Classics these days. She had a faint Eastern European accent, I thought, and a habit of explaining things in too much detail."

Rita shifted her position in the bed a little, not seeing Priya lift her eyebrows when she talked about Olga explaining things too much. Who did that remind Priya of?

Rita had been lying on her back and holding up her iPad. Now she turned to her side, and put it on one of the cushions she had ordered from a shop in Leamington, using photos from her time in Venice. That was something she would miss when she moved back to Leicester. In Leamington she had the benefit of lots of independent shops within walking distance, all offering unusual ideas and services, as well as the convenience of a large H&M, a River Island and an Oliver Bonas shop, all of which were staples for Rita and her friends when looking for clothes or presents. Leicester was a bigger town centre, with more of the large chains, like Zara, but fewer independent stores, and she would have to drive or take the bus to get there.

As she moved, Rita's brown curly hair fell over her face and she pushed it back behind her ears. A new hairdresser was another thing she would have to find, she thought. Thanks to her student discount she had got used to keeping her springy locks under control with the help of Cassie at Pure Hair on Park Street in Leamington, which she had first discovered late one Sunday afternoon when she and her friends had been idly looking in the windows at the properties on offer with various local estate agents. No harm in dreaming, they had thought, and it was interesting to see which areas attracted the highest prices. Overall, the town seemed to be going up in the world from what they had learned, with average house prices over £350,000 and some of the larger properties, often Grade II listed Regency villas, which were beautiful in their elegance Rita had to admit, going for eye watering amounts of well over £1m. Thinking about it now, Rita wondered what effect Brexit would have on the prices; that was another unknown outcome.

"OK, I get the picture" Priya said softly, interrupting Rita's train of thought. "She was unnoticeable except you noticed her." Priya wanted to know more about Rita's encounter with Olga Kelenko. "So, she can't have been that good! What did she want with you anyway?"

"She warned me to be careful." Rita told her.

"Oh Rita!" Priya gasped, "You didn't tell me."

"Well I didn't think much about it at the time. I thought she'd got it wrong to be fair." Rita excused herself.

"So, careful of what?" Priya asked, curling the ends of her hair around her fingers.

"She said there might be money laundering at the trattoria and to be aware of anything unusual happening. I really hadn't spotted anything, and I didn't after our meeting. She was prob'ly mistaken. Anyway, I got on with my work…" Rita said.

.….And getting to know Matteo, thought Priya.

"…And I never saw her again." But, as Rita finished her tale, thoughts were passing through her head which she voiced to her friend. "Now I think back, maybe there were a few things.." Rita shook her head. "I dunno, once you get in that kind of mind everything looks sus doesn't it?" Rita paused, yawning, "It's late" she said, "We really should get some shut eye if we are going to do any work tomorrow."

The friends said goodnight. Rita laid her head on the pillow. She closed her eyes. She counted to 100. It was no good, sleep would not come. Too much screen time her mother would say. Or perhaps it was the exam coming up, or the discussion which Detective Chief Inspector Bridge had booked with her, rather formally she thought, for Monday afternoon. What would he want to know about her time in Venice? Rita tried to produce in her mind an image of the watery city, the fun she had with Matteo, glasses of mint tea at the trattoria on Sunday afternoons. Her eyes felt heavy. She dropped into sleep.

Chapter

5

"Venice is like eating an entire box of chocolate liqueurs in one go."

Truman Capote

Monday 19th June 2017 5.30pm

"What do you remember? Anything unusual?" Detective Chief Inspector Jamie Bridge, the sleeves of his white shirt rolled to the elbows, a blue jacket behind him on the back of his chair, leant towards the screen as if urging Rita to provide some clue, some idea to help take their inquiry forward. His team needed to find out how this woman had ended up in the canal in a pretty poor state. Sympathetic as they felt towards the victim and her family, EMSOU wanted to be sure whether organised crime was involved, in which case it was for them, or whether this was, say, a domestic, which meant they could hand it over to the Leicestershire force. In their short telephone call, Rita had been able to give them a name, which had at least provided their investigations with a focus. Rita, on her return from Warwick to Leamington after their phone conversation on Saturday, had also managed to dig out the business card which Olga had given her while they shared their refreshments in the trattoria to which she had lured the detective. She had scanned it for the DCI to see.

If Olga Kelenko had any secrets, she hid them very well, DCI Bridge's unit was discovering. While Rita had been sitting her exam, specialist teams had been digging, using the information she had provided. Olga Kelenko had no social media presence, not even on Linked-In. With such a relatively unusual name, and an idea of her age, what the team had managed to trace was her education history, her career as a teacher, and a summary of the allegations that had led to her leaving the profession. After that there was nothing. At morning break that day, officers from the Essex police force had visited the school where Olga had taught and spoken to an ex-boyfriend who was on the staff. He had been able to give them an address for her, which the police had then visited at lunchtime.

Jamie Bridge knew from the briefing that the flat where Olga Kelenko had been living was in a place called Epping. His Detective Sergeant had been dispatched there on the first available train as soon as the information from the boyfriend came through. The town turned out to be in Essex, and well-served by transport routes, near to junction 27 of the M25 and close to the start of the M11. The town was also on the tube, at the end of the Central Line. The flat was a rented studio above a clothes shop in the High Street. The town was a pretty, well-heeled place according to his Sergeant, who, having arrived there in the late afternoon, seemed to have acquired most of his local information in the pubs and bars which were scattered along the High Street. Bankers, lawyers and City traders lived there, he reported, hence the air of prosperity, although nearby Epping Forest had a reputation for gangster activity in the past. What was their victim, a private detective operating in Essex, doing in Venice and in Leicester? That was one of the questions they needed to answer. While DS McKenzie enjoyed his takeaway coffee from Panini's Espresso bar, and checked into the Bell Hotel in order to facilitate liaison with the local force, it was urgent that they find out all that Rita knew.

There were details about the body from her post mortem examination which the police had not disclosed, and which the Detective Chief Inspector was not about to share with Rita. There were marks on the woman's arms like cigarette burns, suggesting she might have been tortured, and whoever had put her in the canal had tied her to the shopping trolley. Perhaps they hoped it would sink, or maybe they thought it would serve as a warning. The treatment to which the victim had been subjected pointed to a gang of organised criminals. This was looking less and less like a random act or a domestic argument gone wrong. But what was it she knew that had got her into so much trouble?

Attending the post mortem, the Sergeant had reported to his boss, he had been fearful that the woman was still alive when thrown into the canal. This turned out not to be the case. Yes, she had drowned, but the water in her lungs was the clean and drinkable Severn Trent local tap water, not the dingy liquid that floated in the canal together with plant and animal detritus and all forms of rubbish that human beings chose to toss into it and the conservationists, swimming against the tide as it were, endeavoured to extract. It was mostly plastic bags and small electrical items, but every so often someone would dump something larger, like a fridge, that would involve the Canal Trust, and be reported to the police, although the perpetrators were rarely found. You couldn't put CCTV along the whole of the canal after all. If the magnet fishers, who were not popular with the Canal Trust, had not chosen that spot for their search, Olga Kelenko might never have been found.

The victim's fingerprints hadn't been on the police database so there was nothing to suggest she was involved in the criminal underworld. Ryan Aldred, the ex-boyfriend, was identified by the team as a 'person of interest', for want of any leads, although he seemed a harmless enough geography teacher at a local school in Essex. He had almost fainted when told the news, Sergeant McKenzie had told the briefing meeting on speaker phone. Local inquiries had confirmed what little they had already discovered. The victim had no living family in this country. Her mother had come here from the Ukraine, her father having died there when Olga was ten years old. The circumstances of his death were obscure; there was some suggestion he may have had enemies among Russian emigres who moved to the Ukraine after its independence in 1991, but it was all very murky according to the intelligence sources they had consulted.

Olga had gone to a secondary school in Shenfield, not far from Epping, and graduated from Kings College in London, to which she commuted, apparently, in order to look after her mother, who had died not long after she graduated. Olga had qualified as a Classics teacher, but had switched to teaching Philosophy, Religion and Ethics. She had left teaching to work as a claims investigator. Her ex-boyfriend blamed the false allegations which had led to this career change for also damaging their relationship. He seemed quite sad about it. But he did not seem an angry man and he had no criminal record. He was either innocent or a very good liar.

The search of the victim's flat that afternoon had yielded no files or records, no lap top or other signs that Olga Kelenko conducted any business from there, let alone an investigation business, apart from two large wooden art deco style wardrobes bursting with a variety of outfits suitable for surveillance work – several coats, some overalls, beach wear, cocktail dresses and a selection of skirts, trousers and tops in muted colours. In the sizeable drawers of the matching chest were a variety of hats, scarves and spectacles, not to mention several wigs in different colours. Judging by the videos from the search team, it was like the wardrobe of someone playing a variety of a characters in a domestic play or soap opera.

Significantly, her phone had not been found. When questioned, Ryan Aldred had told them she used an iPhone. Perhaps all her information was stored on that? he had suggested. DCI Bridge's heart had sunk at this news. They would put in the usual request to Apple, of course, and no doubt get the usual rebuff. The company might be profligate with how they disclosed customers' data to third parties, but, when it came to helping the law enforcement authorities, they always refused access on the grounds of breach of privacy. The process of extracting anything could take months.

Jamie Bridge cursed the digital age, when all information which might have been helpful to police inquiries, not only communications but invoices and receipts, were sent electronically. No access to the victim's device or records meant they were denied a way to finding out about her life and, more specifically, how and why she was in Leicester. Local police were trying to fill in some of the gaps by contacting car hire firms, no vehicle having been traced to Olga Kelenko through PNC checks, although she did hold a driving licence. A rented car might have given her anonymity for her inquiries, whatever they were, they reasoned. Since they did not know when she had travelled to the Midlands, or from where, it was premature to examine CCTV on the motorways or at service stations, although that exercise might come once they pieced together her final movements. It was all going to take a lot of time and resources.

"Think if anything unusual happened around the time she met you." the Detective Chief Inspector, trying not to appear desperate to Rita, was clutching at straws.

"Well, I dunno." Rita was sitting with her elbows on her desk, her head resting on her chin as if to stimulate concentration. She wore a check shirt today, over stone washed jeans. Her converse shoes were scattered on the floor where she had left them when the Skype call started. Her hair was tied in the nape of her neck but strands were escaping and springing up around her ears. She had just finished another exam and was feeling pretty tired.

"There was so much happening and it was all new to me." she frowned, suppressing the urge to yawn, "But I did think of a couple of things."

"Mmmn?" Jamie Bridge tried to sound encouraging.

"The day after I got to Venice, to the flat where I was staying, my copy of the Divine Comedy went missing, just for a couple of days. I could have mislaid it when I unpacked, I guess, but I was sure I put it on the table by the bed and when I got back to the room after the orientation meeting it wasn't there. I was like, what? I looked everywhere, but I'm telling you it wasn't in the room. Then, when I got back from my first lecture, there it was, just sitting on the shelf with my other books."

Most officers would have considered this to be a waste of time, and Jamie Bridge was inclined to feel the same, but Rita had helped him with his cases in the past and her instincts were often right. He went with it.

"Why would anyone want that particular book?" he asked, adding "I assume it was in English?"

"Yes" Rita nodded, "I brought the book from England. It was given to me by Siggy, the Registrar's secretary at the university. She said she had been on a study trip with the university herself about 10 years ago and knew how beneficial it was. She had read the Divine Comedy while she was there and recommended that I do so too."

"Oh?" Jamie Bridge thought it sounded an odd choice for holiday reading.

"Dante visited Venice, you know, in early 1321." Rita went on "He came as an ambassador and was a guest of one of the most influential nobles of the time, Giovanni Soranzo was his name. The Soranzo family palace, which is on the right side of the Campo San Polo, has a plaque on it to commemorate Dante's visit. It is a super gothic building." Rita paused to conjure up in her mind's eye the elegant red building with white decoration. "Dante was particularly impressed with the shipyard, the Arsenal, where the Venetians built their fleet," she went on "The ships were so important to the defence of the city that by the second half of the 16th century the Arsenal was like a factory production line, producing

200 ships a month, way more than in other countries at the time. In his poem, Dante used the image of boiling tar, taken from what he had seen there, as a punishment meted out to swindlers. Sadly, Dante's visit to Venice was fatal for him as he caught malaria on the way back and died of it in Ravenna on his return."

Rita went silent for a moment.

"OK" the DCI prompted, trying to be patient while he waited for Rita's enthusiasm for historical facts to abate so they could return to the investigation he was trying to conduct.

Rita shook herself and got back to the point, "I was so upset when I thought the book was missing. I thought I'd have to get a replacement."

"And is this Siggy in the habit of giving books to students?" the DCI asked, texting his Sergeant to get the secretary checked out, just in case.

"I don't know. I didn't ask. It was all last minute. Just before I was due to leave, she called me into the Registrar's office to sort out some paperwork and that's when she gave me the book. I put it in my bag and caught the bus to the airport."

"Right" DCI Bridge thought it was time to move on. The book might be nothing. "Anything else?"

"Well, there was Theeran's dog." Rita told him.

"Come again?" Jamie Bridge thought for a second that maybe this was some complicated mathematical theory, one of those formulae people like to try to crack.

"Theeran is Priya's nephew. You know, Priya Shah, my friend." Rita tried to explain.

The Detective Chief Inspector nodded. It was all coming back to him now. Rita had an extensive network of friends and relations, he recalled, some of whom he had met.

"Well, he's at nursery now, but still likes stuffed toys. I saw this one in a shop in Venice and I thought he would like it. I put it on the bookshelf in my room. When I went to look at it again it was gone and then, a few days later, it was back." she told the DCI.

"And did it look the same? Nothing had happened to it? It was the same dog?" he asked her.

"As far as I could tell. One stuffed dog looks pretty much like another doesn't it?" Rita replied, puzzled.

"And after that? Your studies in Venice finished last December, but you told my Sergeant you made a few trips over there earlier this year?" he pressed.

Rita coughed, embarrassed. "Yes, well, I got to know this guy, Matteo Capetti. I went to see him."

"He didn't come here?" DCI Bridge checked, thinking there might be an immigration record, if the Borders Agency had made a note of his entry.

"No" Rita confirmed quietly.

"And what happened. Are you still seeing him?" DCI Bridge, feeling this sounded rather intrusive when talking to a witness, added, "If you don't mind me asking?"

"No." Rita dropped her head and her voice so he had to strain to hear her. "He dumped me" Rita looked back up at the screen and shrugged her shoulders, "C'est la vie! Or should I say 'e La vita'!"

The Detective Chief Inspector might have sympathised, but at that moment the door to the meeting room where he was sitting opened. He looked over the top of his lap top, prepared to give whoever it was the sharp end of his tongue for interrupting the interview of a vital witness. Except that the person standing in the doorway was his boss, the person who, to everyone's astonishment except hers, had been newly promoted to the rank of Superintendent, Sue Forster.

"Drugs squad" she mouthed, rather than spoke out loud. "We need to talk to them now" she muttered as she pointed over her shoulder with a well-manicured thumb. Her hair, recently dyed blonde, and tied in a pony tail, remained undisturbed against her contrasting dark uniform.

Jamie Bridge nodded.

"I'm sorry Rita" he said, looking at the screen while feeling for his jacket on the back of his chair. "I have to go. We'll continue this when you can get to Leicester. Sergeant McKenzie will make arrangements." The last thing he saw was her puzzled expression as he closed the lap top and headed for his boss's office.

Chapter

6

"All that glisters is not gold"

William Shakespeare,
The Merchant of Venice

Thursday 22nd June 2017 5pm

"It is so good to have you home, Rita." Padma had been standing at the front door of 10 Elm Drive as her daughter's Toyota car pulled up.

Padma had a beaming smile on her face, unable to contain her joy at seeing Rita again, and so unexpectedly. When she had last called her, there had been no hint of this visit. True, there had been that worrying conversation which Nayan had overheard at the weekend. He was sure a police officer at the Infirmary had mentioned Rita's name, but, when Padma had mentioned this, Rita had brushed it off.

Rita hadn't planned on coming back from uni yet. She had intended to wait until she got her results but fate, in the shape of DCI Bridge, had taken a hand. She had used the opportunity to load her car, which she had taken to Leamington this term with the task of emptying the house in mind, with some of the possessions she had accumulated in Brunswick Street over the last two and a half years. There was still a lot left to fetch, which would please her mother who liked to get involved in that sort of thing. She would probably come and check the house was properly clean before the handover to the landlord. Padma had a sharp eye for skirting boards and the inside of kitchen cupboards. Meanwhile, she could see her mother was glad to have her home, and Rita had no intention of explaining the reason for her unplanned visit.

Nayan, walking back from the bus stop, turned the corner into Elm Drive just as Rita was struggling with books in one hand, her blue suitcase on wheels which she was trying to guide with the other, and a Venice cushion jammed under each arm. Nayan took his ear phones out, letting them dangle against his chest where his dark blue T-shirt bore the unexplained legend "I'm in".

"Hi sis" he said as he drifted towards the front door, not offering any assistance but, thinking better of it, he went back and took the suitcase from her.

"Is that you, Nayan?" Padma called from her white and grey kitchen where she had now established herself and where, as Nayan knew she would be, she was preparing a feast fit for a returning daughter.

"Help your sister, will you?" Padma said "She's bringing some of her things back from uni."

Nayan lifted his hands and looked up to the sky. "Oh, my days!" he exclaimed in exasperation. He carried on into the house with the case, left it at the foot of the spiral staircase, and went back to Rita's car, texting his brother as he went "Rita's back. Cum over. Ma's making a feast!"

* * *

"Isn't this nice?" Padma beamed across the table at her three children, giving each a warmed plate. The boys were quickly crunching on pieces of poppadum while they spooned Padma's vegetable curry with coconut milk on to those plates, Rita helping herself to her mother's delicious lime rice. Rita had to concede there were compensations to having to come home early.

"I just thought I'd get ahead of the game" Rita said "Bring some of my stuff home while I wait for the results of my finals"

"Very sensible" Padma said, "And I will help you with the rest when I come to check on the cleaning of the house, so you can get your deposit back. Nayan, you will come and help too."

Rita's younger brother sighed. Here we go, he thought; up against these two women in his family he stood no chance. Mohal, sitting opposite, grinned. He kept his mother short of information on his whereabouts which, as a newspaper reporter, were pretty random; that way it was harder for her to order him about.

Rita's phone was vibrating in her jeans pocket. Probably D S McKenzie finalising arrangements for tomorrow, she thought. She dared not look at her phone. Padma liked to have a 'no phones or tablets' policy at mealtimes.

"I've missed your cooking, Mum" she said, to add to her mother's pleasure further.

"She doesn't cook like this for me." Nayan snorted, helping himself to the rice and getting a rebuking stare from Padma.

"Would you like some more?" Padma asked Rita solicitously, and she gratefully accepted the invitation to another helping. She may as well get into her mother's good books for something; Padma would not be happy if she learnt the real reason for Rita's visit.

"Mohal and I will do the washing up" she said to the surprise of her older brother who she kicked under the table as she said it. Rita wanted to find out what the local paper, the Leicester Mercury, knew about Olga Kelenko's watery demise. It might give her an idea as to what the police wanted to talk to her about. She had some calls to make, too, calls she did not want her mother to hear.

Friday 23rd June 2017 7am

Early the next day, Rita stepped quickly but carefully down the spiral staircase at 10 Elm Drive, holding her pink satchel bag close to her side. It was 7am. Rita was hoping to make it to the front door before her mother heard her.

"Rita? Is that you?" Too late! Her mother's voice came from the master bedroom.

"Just going to meet someone!" she called as she reached the bottom step. Rita was out of the glazed front door before Padma, tying up her dark blue silk dressing gown, could get her head round her bedroom door and call after her. Padma, her grey springy hair sticking up around her head and cascading onto her shoulders, looked up to the ceiling and raised her hands in supplication. What was she supposed to do with such a daughter? She had wanted her children to be independent, but Rita took things too far! Where was she off to at this time of the morning? And without any breakfast. She tutted to herself and went back inside her room to prepare for another day at the dental surgery.

Friday 23rd June 2017 7.45 am

Meera opened the front door as Rita arrived. Priya's older sister was looking blooming again. Her son, Theeran, two years old, or so, Rita thought, was sitting on a dining chair with a booster seat, banging a green plastic spoon into a blue bowl and looking very pleased with himself. Taking in the scene, it seemed to Rita that Meera had left him to this task while she put everything they would need for the day in her car, a silver Ford Fiesta. It was almost as much as Rita had brought home from uni she thought. There was a buggy, a changing mat, various bags which she assumed contained nappies and spare clothes, as well as a box of toys. Meera's stomach had quite a curve; her next baby was due in four months' time. Rita wondered what it would be like packing for two children and dismissed the thought. Maybe Meera and her husband would have to get a bigger car? she mused.

Meera's husband, Jai, a lecturer at Loughborough

University, had been given a research grant to look into the Chinese economy and was on leave from university teaching to pursue his subject, Priya had told Rita. If Meera had thought that might mean more help with the house and the child care, she found the reverse to be the case. Jai had taken a tenancy of a canal-side flat in Leeds "for access to the business school there to get his research done" and drove up and down the M1 in his treasured VW Beetle in order to see his family, mostly at weekends. Meera had not told her parents this. They would not understand and would only worry. She had not told Priya either, until her sister said that Rita wanted to call in. Then Meera had felt she should come clean, but swore Priya to secrecy, and she in turn had sworn in Rita.

"Come on in" Meera said cheerfully, grateful to see another adult face after a restless night with Theeran.

"I put his stuffed dog, the one you gave him, on the shelf in the downstairs bathroom. Have a good look at it, or take it by all means, but don't let Theeran see it or he will want it. He is very attached to his animals. He sees them as little friends, I think. He is still in the tantrum stage, so it's not wise to cross him if it can be avoided. She sighed as the two women walked, one after the other, through the blue front door of the new David Wilson home that Meera and her husband had moved into about 18 months ago. All the houses were brick built and looked pretty similar, Rita had thought, as she had driven through the estate which was called 'Chimes'. It would be easy to get lost there, despite the Satnav, as new buildings and roads were being added all the time. It was lucky that Meera had given her good directions. Rita could see it promised to be a good place to bring up children. There seemed to be green spaces and a little play area with swings.

Now dominated by the university, which was the reason that Meera and Jai had chosen to live there, Loughborough had undergone several changes in its life as a town. The destination of Thomas Cook's first privately chartered railway excursion on 5 July 1851, for many centuries it had been a small market town serving villages in Charnwood Forest and the Soar Valley as well as providing a link by road between London and Derby. The Soar Navigation and the Soar and Trent Canal had brought industry and some prosperity, most notably from the manufacture of worsted, turning the place into an industrial town by the time of the Napoleonic wars.

Expansion had brought dissatisfaction among the growing workforce owing to fluctuations in demand and fortunes. The end of the conflict in Europe led to a big slump and much local suffering. Loughborough was at the heart of demonstrations of workers' frustration, leading to attacks on machinery for which the penalties were severe. It was a harsh time to live, Rita reflected. The power to spread work among the workforce remained with the hosiery masters, while trade unions were banned by the Combination Acts. People were desperate, and there were incidents of frame-breaking in the East Midlands, the most notorious instigator, Ned Ludd, being identified with Anstey, a village in Leicestershire. While the vandalism was generally deplored by the establishment, Lord Byron's was one of the few voices in Parliament to defend the hosiery workers, Rita recalled. He said their extreme actions had arisen from circumstances of the most unparalleled distress.

In this era, John Heathcote had patented a machine to make bobbin lace, revolutionising production on a sort of knitting frame which he called the "Loughborough" frame. He and his partner had set up a mill in Loughborough which was attacked and damaged by the workers. According to reports of the trial of the Luddites, the mill had been like a large factory, containing fifty-five frames.

The attack, which took place just over a hundred years ago, Rita remembered from her history notes, on June 28th to 29th 1816, seemed to have taken the company by surprise and the guards they had placed on duty were easily overcome. Several men, including the ringleader, John Towle, were sentenced to death, while others were transported. The event heralded the end of Luddism in the East Midlands. Meanwhile, Heathcoat refused the offer of £10,000 in compensation, a large sum at the time. Instead, he moved his entire operation to the west country, to the benefit of the town of Tiverton where houses and schools were built by the company for the workers, many of whom, having no other source of work, made the long journey by foot to the new factory from the Midlands.

Throughout history people had moved to places where they hoped to find work or to escape persecution, Rita reflected, but with global newsfeeds now it felt like it was accelerating. Today, people from a number of countries were making hazardous journeys to get to Europe, seeking security and a better life. On-line reports frequently reported asylum seekers and refugees from parts of Africa, where there was religious intolerance, discrimination, or outright war, cramming themselves into lorries, or walking across deserts and inhospitable territories, to get to Libya from where they would make life-threatening boat crossings. Families were fleeing the fighting in Syria, where IS was being repelled, it seemed, but at the horrific expense of the use of barrel bombs and chemical weapons by President Assad against his own people. She had seen on the TV in Venice the number of migrants who were arriving daily in Italy, as well as Greece. It was putting a great strain on resources, yet still local people, able to see the human tragedy which it was, tried to help, while it took a really heartrending story for the desperation of the refugees to reach the national broadcast news. Like the UK's withdrawal from the EU, no one seemed to have any constructive answers.

"Now young man, I think you need a nappy change!" Meera smiled at her son who raised his arms to be lifted out of the chair and was happy to be carried upstairs on what was left of Meera's hip beside her baby bump. He wouldn't get so much attention when the new baby came, Rita thought, as she entered the downstairs bathroom, immaculate with the latest furnishings and lighting. She found the toy dog where Meera had said it would be, looking forlorn on the shelf as if waiting for her. The dog looked exactly as she remembered him, a black and white puppy like those dalmatians in the film. It seemed perfectly normal, no signs of anything untoward apart from a slightly chewed ear which she took to be the work of Theeran. It hadn't been chewed when she bought it. Still, she would take it with her, since Meera had offered.

"Thanks, Meera'''" she called up the stairs, "Have a good day!" For the second time that morning, Rita left a house before the occupant could say goodbye properly.

Friday 23rd June 2017 8.45 am

Rita called Priya when she got to Hinckley Road police station, which was where she had been asked to report. At least there was somewhere to park. If they had sent her to a central station like Belgrave Road that would have been more difficult. The building was not very inspiring she thought. It was like a large brick house with too few windows and a yard at the back with a secure gate. It was all a bit off-putting. It was 8.45 and she was fairly sure that Priya would be awake. Hadn't she said something about going out that day? Wasn't she going on another boat trip? She seemed to spend all her revision breaks on water these days.

"Glad you got a new phone." Rita said when Priya answered, "Mission accomplished."

"You have ze dog?" Priya tried a pretend Russian accent. "Taking it for walkies?"

"Ha ha" said Rita, "Where are you going today?"

"Oh, we're going punting on the Cherwell river, again, but with a professional this time." Priya told her. "He dresses like a gondolier and takes you wherever you want to go on the river. We're taking a picnic."

Rita, instantly picturing the skilled boatmen on the water in Venice, thought she liked the sound of Priya's day more than her own. Better get it over with she thought as the pair said their goodbyes.

Friday 23rd June 2017 9am

"Would you state your name and date of birth for the tape please?"

Rita coughed self-consciously. She had hardly sat down before this request was made. It did not exactly put her at ease. Rita complied.

"Thank you. I am Detective Constable Devinder Singh from the East Midlands Specialist Operations Unit. I work with DCI Bridge." An attractive Asian man, wearing a blue and white check shirt and navy cargo trousers, which had large pockets on each leg, smiled across the grey meeting table at Rita. He had a line of beard hugging his chin and a blue turban on his head. He looked to be in his mid-twenties, about Mohal's age she thought. Taking in the room as she had entered, the station seemed to have had a bit of a make-over since she had last been inside. The walls looked like they had been painted recently, and the meeting table and chairs looked relatively new. There was even a pot plant in the corner. Rita couldn't tell whether or not it was real.

"And I am Detective Constable Dominic Fryer." said the other man who was looking at her. His beard was thicker and he was casually dressed in an orange and black check shirt and black jeans – was this the new police force Rita wondered? "I'm from the drugs squad." he was saying as Rita looked down at her own, much smarter, clothes which she had donned that morning in order to be taken seriously – a white shirt with her grey NEXT trouser suit.

The police officers were sitting back in their chairs, looking relaxed, pens and paper on the table, like confident examinees waiting to be told to turn over the questions. Rita was sitting forward, leaning towards them and, in spite of her mother's advice, had her elbows on the table. Rita nodded at the officers and reached into her pink satchel bag which was on the plastic chair next to her. She took out the stuffed dog and placed it on the table between herself and the two policemen.

The officers raised their eyebrows in synchrony and sat up properly, paying attention at last.

"Now Rita you're not going to confess, are you?" Dominic Fryer had a strong Southern Irish accent. He was on secondment from the Garde to the National Crime Agency, NCA for short, to gain more experience in policing international drug smuggling. Since the UK had voted to leave the European Union, and since the outcome of any Brexit negotiations, which had barely started, even though the Prime Minister had served the Article 50 notice earlier in the year, was uncertain, no one knew what the border arrangements between Northern Ireland and Ireland would be in 2019. The authorities in Ireland had therefore decided to beef up drug enforcement, and learn more about international drug smuggling, by seconding police officers to England.

Rita, who had opened her mouth to speak, closed it again and began nervously to fiddle with the topknot into which she had pinned her hair that morning.

"No, of course not!" she said indignantly.

"Only we'd have to caution you if y'are." DC Fryer continued, looking straight into her eyes.

"It was just that Inspector Bridge" Rita could not get used to calling him Chief Inspector, "said to think about anything unusual that happened in Italy. Well, first there was Dante's Divine Comedy and then there was this." Rita gestured to the dog who sat mournfully on the table.

"Dante's Comedy?" DC Singh looked perplexed. His colleague sat back in his chair and turned to him; he had seen a copy of Rita's discussion with DCI Bridge, he had got this.

"She was given a copy. She lost it. She found it again." he told him, then, turning to Rita, "That's about right isn't it?"

"Yes" said Rita, displacing strands of hair from her top knot. "And.."

"And the same thing happened to the dog." Detective Constable Fryer interrupted, taking his pen and using it to poke at the dog gently.

"That's right" Rita confirmed, wondering how he knew this.

"And you bought the dog for…" Dom Fryer consulted his notes, "a baby called Feeron?"

"Theeran" Rita corrected him, aware now that her hair-do was disintegrating and trying to retrieve it while she spoke. It had been a mistake to fiddle with the clip, she thought.

"He's two. Years old I mean." she told the two men opposite her. "The nephew of my best friend. Well, soon there will be a new nephew or niece as Meera, Priya's sister, is pregnant…" Rita came to a halt, aware that the police officers were politely waiting to put their next question.

"We know about the dog." DC Fryer poked at him in a friendly way again.

Dev Singh nodded his turbaned head wisely in agreement, although Rita was not sure how much he really did know.

"You see, Rita," Dominic Fryer managed to say her name as if the third letter was a 'd' not a 't', which she found disconcerting, "The National Crime Agency have had the trattoria on our radar for a time – the one below the flat where you stayed. We saw you buy the dog."

Rita opened her mouth again, this time in astonishment. She had been followed in Venice, not only by Olga Kelenko but also by the NCA? she thought indignantly. No wonder the city's streets were teeming with people, if everyone was being watched by at least two others, it made perfect sense.

"We took it a few days before you were due to leave. We tested it and it had about half a kilo of cocaine in it, street value of £25,000."

Rita looked at the stuffed dog with new eyes. Theeran had played with him, he had chewed his ear. What if…?

"Don't worry." DC Fryer reassured her, while his colleague was scribbling notes. How much of this had DC Singh known before this? she wondered.

"We let the dog through Customs and we left it with you to be collected." Dominic Fryer went on.

"Collected?" Rita croaked in surprise, "What do you mean?" Rita did not like the sound of this. She had unwittingly smuggled cocaine into the country and the police had let her? She had brought cocaine into her mother's house that Christmas holiday? Where she had wrapped the dog before giving it to Priya for her nephew? No, wait a minute, Priya had been implicated in this too?

"Rita, your brain is working so fast I can almost hear the cogs whirring." DC Fryer leant towards her and poured her a glass of water using the tall container on the table.

"It went down like this." he said. Rita watched DC Singh hold his pen at the ready. He would have a lot to report to his Chief Inspector when they next met Rita thought.

"How did you get back from the airport when you left Venice at the end of your course?" DC Fryer asked. Rita reflected for a moment.

"By bus" she said. "Several of us travelled together on the plane to Birmingham and then we got the Megabus to Leamington. You don't mean the dog was swapped back then? While it was in my baggage on the bus?"

Devinder Singh was about to nod but Dominic Fryer shook his head, so he stopped and examined his pen instead before proceeding to write again.

"No" the Irishman said, "What happened when you got back to the house in Brunswick Street, Rita?"

Rita looked into the middle distance, not seeing either of the men opposite her while she recalled that evening.

"My housemates were glad to see me. I was pleased to see them too. There was literally no one on the course in Venice who I made particular friends with, they just weren't my type." Rita could see the officers were losing interest, she shook her head and continued, "It was just at the end of the autumn term. I put my bags down in my room and we went straight out to eat at the Millennium Balti in Bath Street" she said. "We had a great night!" Rita's eyes sparkled at the memory of the reunion. It had been good to get back together with her old friends after a whole term away in a strange environment.

"And when you got back?" Dominic Fryer raised his eyebrows questioningly.

"Well, nothing really" Rita said slowly, puzzled. "Oh" she said, remembering there was something.

"When we got back to the house and went through the door, we noticed there was a draught coming in. It was a cold night. Everyone thought the windows had been shut before we left but, when we checked, one of the windows to Sammi's room downstairs was half open. We closed the sash and looked around. Some cash had gone – we were always saying don't leave money lying around. I had a feeling that my cases weren't exactly where I had left them, but I couldn't be sure. We didn't report it. The police don't investigate burglaries these days, do they? And it was only cash. That seemed strange. None of the lap tops or bikes were touched. It was a relief, really, some people had about a term's work on their computers. So that was when…?"

Rita was realising that, while she and her friends had been having a celebratory curry, the dog with drugs inside had been exchanged for the dog she had first bought. Then another thought occurred to her, "And you were watching the house? You saw who did it?"

"Ah, to be sure, I can't disclose that" Dominic Fryer said enigmatically. "Let's just say it's a line of inquiry." Both DCs nodded sagely. They paused a moment, DC Singh to review the notes he had made so far, DC Fryer to allow Rita's thoughts to collect together.

"Oh" Rita's hand went to her mouth. "Well I went to Venice several times after that. Tell me it hasn't happened again!"

Chapter

7

"There is no greater sorrow than to recall happiness in times of misery."

Dante Alighieri

Friday 23rd June 2017 4.30pm

Padma was getting anxious. At the dental surgery in Uppingham Road, Anita, the new receptionist, frowned as her employer peered furiously at her phone and paced up and down in front of her. The patients would pick up on her anxiety, Anita thought. The practice was meant encourage them to feel calm.

"Where is Rita? Why won't she answer? I've left a dozen messages. Can you call her for me?" Padma asked Anita, "It might just be me she's avoiding."

Anita, who thought this was a fuss about nothing, jumped down from her chair and emerged from behind the white curved reception desk to check Rita's number. Patients who had only seen Anita behind the desk from the waist up were always amazed the first time they saw her. Measuring 1.24 metres in height, she had achondroplasia, a form of dwarfism.

Anita had not let her condition interfere with her life. She had fought her way into and through mainstream school and defied her teachers and her parents to achieve good passes at GCSE and A Level. Since then she had held down various jobs, when people were willing to give her a chance. The receptionist job at the surgery was a bit of a stop-gap. It suited her because it was local- she had a flat not far away in Humberstone- and there was a disabled parking space near the surgery where she could leave her red Fiat Punto which had been adapted for her to drive.

Anita was thinking of studying for a qualification in Human Resources and was intending to ask Padma if she could work part-time to fit in her studies. She needed to keep her boss happy, so she smoothed down her skirt, tucked her long fair hair behind her ears, and made the call. Not surprisingly, and to Padma's increased distress, there was no answer, only Rita's voicemail. "Rita Patel. Reading history and solving mysteries. Leave a message and if it's interesting I'll call you back." Anita didn't think there would be anything to be gained by adding to Padma's messages.

It was just before 5pm. The last of the day's patients were arriving, apprehensive about their treatment and more nervous when they saw the agitated look on Padma's face. Anita was glad when Dr Sharma stepped out of his surgery,following an older man, a patient who was carefully exploring the inside of his mouth with his tongue.

"Give it a couple of hours before you eat anything or have a hot drink." Dr Sharma said. "Otherwise you're good to go. Anita will sort out your paperwork."

Dr Sharma, as calm and reassuring as Padma was alarming, smiled at his patient, took in the scene at the desk, and said, "Anything wrong?" indicating with a gesture of his hand that Padma might want to enter his surgery for a quiet word.

Padma followed him, shaking her head as she went. While Caroline, the dental nurse, cleared up the surgery after the last patient and prepared for the next one, Padma filled Dr Sharma in on her latest concerns about Rita.

"She left so early. Wouldn't say where. Now she won't answer her phone. I don't know where she is!" Padma threw her hands in the air and let them land with a slap on her thighs.

"Well I have a filling to do" Dr Sharma said carefully, "and you have a couple of children's check-ups." he said, trying to get Padma to concentrate on what she could control and what she could not, the latter also known as her daughter Rita.

"After that I will try to contact Rita myself. She won't be far away I am sure." he said firmly, even though what little contact he had had with Rita, and the stories he had heard about her, rather led him to think the opposite.

Friday 23rd June 2017 5.30 pm

Half an hour later and Dr Sharma, having ushered out his last patient, was staring at the message on his phone and wondering what to do about it. He had sent Rita a text from his own phone. He had her number stored from the days when his wife had been killed in a burglary and Rita had helped to look after his children.

"I'm at Hinckley Road Police Station" the reply said, "Helping with inquiries!"

Dr Sharma did not like the sound of that, but thought the news would only distress Padma further. He put on his jacket and switched off the surgery light. Pointing to the door of Padma's surgery, where she was still conducting check- ups on a set of twin nine-year olds, he turned to Anita and said "Tell Padma I know where Rita is. I'm going to see her."

Friday 23rd June 2017 6.30pm

Dr Sharma entered through the automatic doors of the police station on Hinckley Road. He couldn't see any police officers. Walking up to the desk, he waited for a minute, then noticed a bell with an arrow pointing at it. A drawing from an edition of Alice's Adventures in Wonderland that he had been reading to his children came into his mind; it was of a bottle that said 'drink me' on it. He pressed as invited. After a few minutes there was movement, and a young woman appeared at the counter, her face partly hidden by the plastic screen until she pushed it aside. It felt like he had wandered into a Post Office by mistake, one of those hybrid places which hide at the end of shops, among the washing up liquids and tins of beans. Doctor Sharma gave Rita's name.

"I'll go and check" the young woman said, "Take a seat." she vanished but ,unlike the Cheshire Cat in the book, she left behind no smile.

Dr Sharma looked around him, passing his hand over his oiled head of hair. Perhaps the station resembled a jobcentre he thought, or a collection point in Argos. There were several stands with leaflets on various subjects, such as where to find drug addiction clinics, local alcoholics anonymous meetings and a number for the Samaritans. On the walls were posters explaining what numbers to call depending on the emergency. There were two rows of hard chairs for visitors, bolted to the ground. A middle-aged man in a grey suit was lying across three of the seats. He seemed to be asleep judging by the snoring.

Dr Sharma did not have long to take in the scenery, but he was shocked by what he saw next. Coming towards him was a trembling and tearful Rita, escorted by two men in check shirts, dark trousers and yellow Doc Martin boots. It was only their ID badges swinging against their chests which suggested these were police officers. What was going on?

Friday 23rd June 2017 7.15pm

Back in his own home, Dr Sharma was getting death stares from his mother in law, Chanda, who, while he had been collecting Rita, had put his two children to bed. Was it not enough that he had brought her daughter to this so-called civilised city where she had been brutally murdered, her look seemed to say, without then bringing home a vulnerable and emotionally disturbed young woman? She based this judgement on the fact that Rita was sitting on the black sofa, curled up almost in a foetal position, the box of tissues she had given her clutched on her lap as if it contained precious jewels. Staring hard at her son in law again, she went out to make some tea.

"Rita likes peppermint" her son in law called after her. He was not sure she had heard.

Dr Sharma had never seen Rita in such a state before. He was glad his children were asleep upstairs and not witnesses to this.

He had driven her to his house in his own car, not trusting her to be in any state to drive her own, and not wanting to take her to Padma's until she had calmed down a bit. Rita had said very little on the journey as he navigated through the traffic to Melton Road, from which his house in Syston, to the north east of the city, could be reached by a couple of turns. She sobbed intermittently and sometimes sniffed. He had lent her his cotton handkerchief, carefully ironed by his mother in law, and by the time they arrived it was a soggy creased ball of material which his wife's mother had extracted from her hands in return for the tissue box.

The two male police officers who had been with Rita had seemed relieved to see that there was someone waiting for her and had been keen to hand her over as quickly as possible. Whatever they had said to her they had not expected this reaction, it seemed.

"We'll be in touch" was the last thing one of them had said. Dr Sharma did not think this sounded like a good idea.

The tea arrived, but Rita did not notice. Chanda signalled to her son in law. Should she stay or go? He indicated 'go' and put his hands together and bowed as if to say 'thanks'. She left, giving him a final death stare as she departed.

"I'm sorry" Rita sobbed, seeming only now to realise where she was. "You don't want me here dripping all over your sofa." She took a deep breath and straightened herself up a bit.

Above the fireplace her eyes met a painting of the Rialto Bridge. Venice had been a favourite place of Dr Sharma and his wife. It was where they went after their wedding. A storm of sobbing overtook Rita again as tears ran down her face and her breathing came in uneven waves. She battled to control herself.

"Sorry" she said again, shaking her curly hair which had come loose somewhere on the drive to Dr Sharma's house. Her white top had stains on it that looked like drops of tea. She had sat so long in the interview room that her grey trousers needed a press. She had thrown the jacket on the sofa in a gesture of despair but Dr Sharma had collected it up and carefully folded it beside her. He thought the creation of order might help bring Rita to her senses.

Rita made another effort and took a deep breath.

"I'm sorry" she repeated, "It's just been such a shock. No one likes being made a fool of." To Dr Sharma's consternation her tears and wailing started again. Dr Sharma wished she would cry more quietly. His mother in law would be listening from the study next door while pretending to read her book.

"Is there anyone...?" Dr Sharma began, casting around in his mind for who might be most suitable to comfort Rita right now, and maybe find out what it was the police had said that had so upset her.

He went through the options; not her mother, Rita needed to collect herself before she saw Padma or she would never let her daughter out of her sight again, not her brothers, who were lovely guys but not equipped for this. Her best friend Priya would be the first choice, but he knew from what Padma had said that Priya was still in Oxford.

"Do you mind if I look at your phone?" he asked Rita and received a confirmatory shrug of her shoulders. He didn't like rooting in her pink satchel bag, but if she wasn't going to proffer the phone, he would have to find it himself. It wasn't buried too deep.

"The code is 1485" Rita told him between sobs.

Of course, he thought to himself, Rita's obsession with the Battle of Bosworth and Richard III! He might not know much British history but thanks to Rita he knew that date.

Dr Sharma scrolled through Rita's contacts. Her uni housemates would be in Leamington he thought. The young woman she would be sharing a flat with after she graduated, Morwenna Maitland, had gone abroad after her final exams. Padma had told him that. He was running out of ideas. Then he hit on it. Just the right person, if only she was around. Tentatively he pressed the screen and waited for a reply.

Chapter

8

"Though there are some disagreeable things in Venice, there is nothing so disagreeable as the visitors."

Henry James

Saturday 24th June 2017 9am

A strange light was glimmering though the curtains and flashing against the backs of Rita's eyes. Still more than half asleep, Rita pictured the Diwali ball she had been to with Matteo in Venice, early in their relationship. She had wondered then how he had afforded it. There were lots of wealthy people there, men in well-cut evening suits, and women in sequinned evening dress, their thin figures weighed down with jewellery at their throats and wrists. It was more like a Bollywood dream sequence than the Diwali parades and fairs she was used to on the streets of Leicester, everyone in the crowds wrapped up against the November weather on the 'Golden Mile' along Belgrave Road. She had also missed out on the more low-key celebrations in Leamington, when the decorative lights went on in the Parade, the main street at the heart of the town. The lights declared 'Happy Diwali' at one end and 'Happy Christmas' at the other. It sort of reflected modern Britain, she felt.

The ball in Venice was more of a society event, and had no real religious significance, in the same way that people of all beliefs and none hold or attend Christmas parties, Rita supposed. She had had to look hard among the remaining locals in Venice to find any people like herself, not just English but of Indian origin with a Hindu background, albeit that her grandparents had come to the UK from

Uganda, bringing her parents with them as children. There had been little migration from India to Italy, she was aware, and, according to what she had read, there were only about 170,000 Hindus in Italy altogether, most of whom were to be found in the northern cities. This was another case of population movements brought about by industrial and technological changes, she thought. They had brought their agricultural skills with them, which they had put to good use in the manufacture of mozzarella and parmesan, although the majority involved in cheese production were Sikhs rather than Hindus, Rita had learned, and had passed this information on in a tweet hoping Sammi would see it and respond, which he did "#bestcheesemakers." The Italian government had only granted Hinduism official recognition, alongside Buddhism, as recently as 2012, apparently, although a number of temples and gudwaras had been built in the country by the migrants from India who settled there.

The ball had been lively, with an abundance of food, and alcohol for those who wanted it, and too many rich people showing off in a rather exaggerated way, probably fuelled by drugs, she now realised. Swirling yellow lights had swept across the crowd and lit up the dancers on the stage who were leading them in well-known sequences from Bollywood movies, everyone stepping and swaying in time, their arms aloft or lowered to be clapped together in time to the music.

Rita's eyes flickered open a little. Where was she? Not on the dance floor, the bedsheets made that clear. There was light coming through a window next to the bed, light made yellow by the daffodil pattern printed on the curtains. Rita struggled to recall where she was and how she had got here. This was not her room, either at Elm Drive in Oadby or in Brunswick Street in Leamington.

She remembered something. "It's the sense of betrayal" Athena Maitland had said between gritted teeth as she had determinedly pulled the yellow duvet over Rita's prone body the previous evening, treating her like a small child.

"That's what's hard to get over. Sleep well" and she had switched off the lamp and left the room.

Saturday 24th June 2017 10am

"To want a better past is to fail to forgive yourself" Athena advised her as they sat over brunch that morning, a mixture of lactose free yoghurt and meat free bacon, washed down with matcha green tea. It was not Rita's favourite food, but she didn't really care what she ate at that moment. It was thoughts and ideas that were gnawing away inside her, not hunger pains. After taking a shower almost automatically, not really thinking what she was doing, she was wrapped in one of Athena's kimonos, which was white with pictures of peacock feathers in black and pink. She had a pair of pink towelling slippers on her feet. Athena had found them for her in a drawer. She had kept supplies of toiletries and slippers for the guests she used to have at the bed and breakfast business she ran in the house, which was situated in the Knighton district of Leicester. Rita's shirt was washed and on a hanger by the kitchen door, her suit was still in the room where she had spent the night.

"This Matteo, the police think he was in on it?" Athena asked her as she sipped at her tea. Rita nodded.

"What a creep!" Athena exclaimed, banging her cup back in its saucer. "Plenty more fish in the sea." Athena was full of aphorisms today.

The last time Rita had seen the woman, who had employed Rita and Priya, when they were younger, to clean and generally help out with the bed and breakfast guests, had been after Rita had been through a bit of trauma. Athena, who usually looked so well-groomed had then looked like she had been through battles too. Her neatly maintained auburn hair, worn at shoulder length, had been replaced by what could only be described as a 'chop'. Her hair had been short, with bits sticking out, and it was a strange purple colour, Rita recalled. She also had several piercings in her ears, eyes and nose. The old Athena would never have entertained those. She seemed to have been transformed from Buddhist to punk by her husband's abrupt departure from their marriage.

That experience would explain some of the advice she was giving, Rita thought. Now the woman across the table from her appeared to be transitioning back towards her previous, composed, self. Her hair was short but in a smooth style, reaching just past her ears, and a light brown colour, more suitable for her age, which must be somewhere in the fifties Rita thought. Looking around the spacious pine kitchen, where Athena had entertained guests at breakfast and also, although this wasn't really part of the business, sustained them with wholesome vegetable soups in the evening, Rita saw several boxes which presumably were packed with kitchen equipment. There was a buyer for the house, which Athena and her husband had dubbed 'Sundial' in honour of the sundial in the centre of the front drive. Athena was preparing to move on, Rita gathered.

"The sale has come at a good time, really." Athena was trying to see the upside. "It meant we could give Morwenna money towards a flat. The one you will both be sharing soon." Rita nodded, embarrassed at being the beneficiary of this windfall.

"And where are you moving to?" Rita asked her.

"Totnes" Athena replied to her surprise, naming a town in Devon. "I want to make a new start." she explained. "Morwenna doesn't need me around so much, and Totnes has lots of independent businesses. I'm taking over a tea shop which has a good sized flat above and a meditation room in the garden. I am getting into mindfulness now. I might run some groups." Rita was pleased to hear her friend and former employer sounding so positive. A move to the west country-it put Rita in mind of Heathcote a hundred years ago and how he had moved his business from Loughborough to Tiverton.

"What about you, Rita?" Athena extended a sympathetic hand across the pine table to touch Rita's arm.

"I'll mend" she shrugged, but her eyes were straying far away as she thought back to her time in Venice with Matteo. That she, Rita Patel, solver of mysteries, should have been taken in, that was what hurt the most. It was starting to make her feel angry. She had been so stupid.

In the course of the previous day, the interview was as interrupted by breaks as a cricket match in damp weather, a fact Rita had learned from a previous boyfriend. The officers from the Organised Crime Unit and the National Crime Agency had gone over her time in Venice in painstaking detail. Where did you go? What did you buy to bring home? How did you travel? All the strange things that had happened in Italy, the things that went missing and turned up again, the way her possessions had been disturbed while she was at lectures, she had put down to her own carelessness or lack of attention, or to the cleaners at the Italian flat. She had never for one moment thought there was a pattern to them.

Then there were the odd things that had happened when she got back to the UK. Why had she not seen what was going on? Was she too blinded by her infatuation with Matteo? Was she too busy with her uni work, too focussed on getting her dissertation in on time? According to the detectives, there were several items she had brought into the UK which had been allowed through Customs even though the authorities knew they contained cocaine. The aim was to observe how the items with the drugs inside were replaced with the originals once safely in the country, and to use the intelligence collected to disrupt the operations of whoever was circulating those drugs in England. By allowing the cocaine to go through, it was hoped the gang – a gang for which she now knew Matteo worked- would not be alerted.

It was a branch of the Mafia, most likely, the officers had told a wide-eyed Rita, possibly the Ndrangheta from Calabria, who were spreading their net further, operating across international borders and almost impossible to stop.

"He may not have had a choice" the police officers had told Rita, "He may have been under pressure himself." Somehow that did not make her feel any better. It seemed to her that she had been one of many victims, and that even now he was probably preying on some other innocent idiot who trusted him and did not see past the charm to notice what he was really doing.

"We cut off one route, they develop another." the Detective Constables had told her. But Rita hadn't been listening. The items where drugs had been hidden, according to the officers, travelled through her mind like prizes on the conveyor belt of the game show from the 70s which she had seen on a Bruce Forsyth tribute programme. It always ended with a cuddly toy, she gathered. A cuddly toy had been the first item used by the smugglers. It did all make sense now, the gifts that had been showered on her, and the shopping trips which Matteo had encouraged. There had been cushions she took a shine to as gifts for Priya and for Padma, a handcrafted jewellery box which Matteo insisted she have; he even gave her a new cabin bag which, she realised, must have had a false bottom. Rita had been taking a huge risk, unknowingly, every time she left Italy. How Matteo and his friends must have laughed at her, and how they must have mocked the authorities, thinking they had got away with it.

It explained the break-in at the Leamington Spa house, the fact that on her way back after the Carnivale trip her suitcase seemed to have been messed about with before it appeared on the carousel, and, after a long weekend in Venice in March, when she and Matteo had a romantic trip on a gondola piloted by a friend of his, she remembered that the taxi driver,who Matteo had arranged to pick her up from

Birmingham airport – "he's a friend" he had told her- had dropped her luggage on the pavement and scrambled to reassemble it. All those incidents were the gang collecting their drugs when they arrived in the country, substituting identical goods for those she had bought. Matteo must have double backed on their shopping outings and bought duplicates, she thought, to be shipped out to contacts in the Midlands so they could make the swaps.

"A lot of Mafia members are pressurised into criminal activity. It's a way of life in some places." It was at that point in the interview that Rita had begun to shake and from then things got worse as the items and the incidents were examined in close detail until she reached the state in which Dr Sharma had witnessed her at the police station.

Rita stared down at her meat-free bacon. You can't trust anyone she thought angrily, her mouth tightening. The phrase acted like a switch in her brain. Don't trust anyone. Those had been the words of Olga Kelenko. Was that why she ended up in the canal? Rita, recovering at last from the initial shock, was starting to feel more like herself. Athena could see this change.

"Come on" she said, pushing back her chair to stand, "Let's clear up then I'll run you to your car."

"Thanks" said Rita distractedly, part of her brain trying to work out how she could get information on who Olga Kelenko had spooked so much in Leicester that they wanted her dead.

Chapter

9

*"This was Venice, the flattering and suspect beauty-
this city, half fairy tale half tourist trap."*

Thomas Mann

Sunday 25th June 2017 2pm

"Skydiving!?" Priya could not believe what Rita had just said
"<u>You</u> are going skydiving?" Rita's friend's emphasis on the
word 'you' fully demonstrated her incredulity at this news.
Priya's trips to the gym and occasional games of badminton
sounded tame by comparison, she was thinking.

Priya had called to distract Rita from the melancholy she
had sensed around her last time they spoke. It seemed that
Padma had had the same idea. While as a mother she was
not happy with the concept of her offspring jumping out of
aeroplanes, Nayan had been nagging to do something like
that for ages. Glider flying was out of reach for the present,
he realised, from a cost point of view and because it would
make too big a dent in his study and work time. But skydiving
was far cheaper and quicker to arrange and could be done
at the local airport, which was only a few miles from their
home, as he told his mother cheerfully. Then Padma had
the thought that, if Rita went too, it would mean someone
would stop him from killing himself in his enthusiasm, and
it might help Rita to snap out of her gloom. She knew her
younger children well enough to realise they both had a
taste for risk and danger, although she had no idea where it
came from. Maybe this would be a way of channelling it in
a safe way. After all, there would be instructors and lots of
safety measures, she reasoned. It was probably less risky than

crossing the road.

"I'll be fine." Rita shrugged, feigning nonchalance. She did not sound too keen. "I don't think it will be too bad. I am going to keep Nayan company. Heights aren't really my thing."

"But you'll be ok?" Priya was hoping her friend might say more.

"Of course. You jump in tandem with an instructor, so nothing can really go wrong." Rita delivered her reply in a deadpan voice.

"Well, there's plaque on a wall in my college, on Deadmans Walk, you know, the route near Christchurch Meadow where the Jewish population would walk when they were taking the bodies of the deceased to their cemetery…" Priya was trying to engage Rita's interest in history.

"Oh yeh." Rita responded with an uncharacteristic failure of curiosity.

"Well, the plaque is to James Sadler, the first English Aeronaut." Priya pressed on.

"How come?" Rita stirred herself to show a little interest.

"He made a successful ascent in a fire balloon near that spot in October 1784." Priya told her.

"He must have been brave," Rita responded, recalling how nervous she had been on her first and only balloon trip not so long ago, and that was with all the health and safety regulations that apply these days, she thought, "How far did he get?"

"The balloon is said to have gone up to 3600 feet and he travelled about 6 miles, to a place called Wood Eaton." Priya was pleased to be the one supplying information to Rita for a change.

"How come he knew about hot air balloons?" Rita queried.

"He worked as a lab technician in the chemistry department, apparently, and experimented with small gas balloons there. He made another, even more successful trip, in November of the same year. This time he took off in a hydrogen balloon from the Botanic Garden in Oxford and got as far as Aylesbury in about twenty minutes!"

"Gosh!" was all that Rita could muster.

"That's much quicker than the 280 bus, by the way." Priya laughed, "He lived to be 75 so he must have known what he was doing." Getting no response, she pressed on, "There is another plaque recording his exploits at the church of St Peter in the East, which is part of St Edmund Hall now; that's where his gravestone is."

"Fancy." Rita managed to say.

Priya was feeling that it might take more than historic ballooning exploits to do the trick of cheering Rita up. She tried another subject.

"The NHS will be 70 soon!" Priya tried.

"I guess" Rita was still not really engaged in the conversation, which they were conducting on Facetime, Rita from her room at Elm Drive, Priya from hers in Oxford.

"I don't think the founders envisaged the sort of thing we see now." Priya told her, drawing on her weeks of experience in various departments of the Oxford University Hospitals Trust to prepare for the clinical part of her training, which would begin soon, if she passed her exams well enough.

"Most patients have multiple problems, sometimes caused by lifestyle." Priya told her friend.

"Such as?" Rita realised she needed to make an effort.

"Obesity mainly. Lots of type 2 diabetes. Smoking that leads to lung cancer and makes other conditions like heart attacks and strokes more likely, alcohol abuse causing liver and gall bladder problems, and, of course, drug taking. It's not just young addicts, it's the middle-aged social users. They are from the hippy generation when the drugs were less strong. They don't realise how potent today's drugs. Then there are people getting comatose on SPICE, and drug users stealing to feed their habit and attacking others in the process, with weapons and even using acid. We see the effects of these attacks on the streets. What's really horrible is to see is how young the people are who are caught up in these things. Often, it's youngsters from poor estates and children excluded from school. It's as if gangs have replaced their communities, their sense of identity."

"Yeh. Gang mentality is evil" Rita said, thinking again about Matteo and the criminals he had got caught up with. Gangs were not a new thing. In the early days of Venice, you risked your life to move across the bridges from one Square to another. People had to keep to their own part of the city or fights would break out. The gangs recognised one another by the colour of their hats or the side on which their women wore their flowers. It was just like the postcode gangs in England. Really, society was not getting any better, Rita sighed to herself.

She must shake off these feelings of sadness and regret, she told herself. But being reminded by her friend about the problems of drug use was not helping. "Each century has its own health problems I suppose." Rita said, turning to the history side of medicine for solace, it was a subject she had studied and which she knew would interest Priya. "The industrial revolution brought cholera and other illnesses to the towns until public health measures were taken. There were accidents in the new factories all the time until the law started to require safe working conditions and shorter hours for children. Going further back, the trade routes brought outbreaks of the plague which have been a serious threat at various times in history." she observed.

"That's what you studied in Venice wasn't it?" Priya asked, hoping that history might be the key to lifting her friend's spirits after all.

"Yes," Rita wriggled to a better position, feeling more alert now an interesting topic had arisen. "Venice had lots of outbreaks of plague. The worse was around 1575 when about

50,000, a third of the population, died."

"And what was causing it?" Priya indulged her friend, although she also had studied medical history. "They used to think it was rats on ships, didn't they?"

Rita nodded. "Yes, modern research suggests it was simply spread by human contact, through lice mainly, thanks to the opening up of trade routes such as the Silk Road." she explained. "Venice was pre-eminent for trade with the East until a sailing route via Cape Horn was discovered, so it was particularly susceptible. Its importance declined around the time of the outbreak of the Black Death in the 1630s, which decimated the city. The Venetians saw the illness as a punishment from God, but they did develop clever ideas to stop it spreading." Rita was warming to her subject now.

"The Venetian City Council invented quarantine, banning newcomers from entering the harbour for forty days. They also designated areas for disposal of the victims and areas to which the dying should be moved. Statistics show these steps reduced the impact the plague might otherwise have had on Venice. Populations in the surrounding Ottoman Empire were not so protected and suffered tremendous losses as a result."

"Of course, there are three kinds of plague." Rita went on.

"Bubonic, pneumonic and septicaemia" Priya could not help putting in "The first is a bacterial toxin transmitted by animals, the second is a bacterial infection affecting the lungs which may be spread by droplets in the air from victims and animals, and the third is a life-threatening infection of the blood probably caused by bites." she summarised. "The Black Death was so named because extremities like the nose would get gangrene. Another common symptom was lumps in the groin and armpits."

"Charming!" said Rita, chuckling now, Priya was pleased to note, "Thank goodness for antibiotics." she added.

"Yes, but they are getting less effective as you know. We

need to restrict their use or there will a return of illnesses we can't cure." Priya told her.

"When the plague struck, the people must have thought that their judgment day had come." Priya sympathised. "The plague was in England, too, wasn't it?" she remembered from their history lessons.

"Oh yes," Rita agreed. "We have a great description of an early outbreak in Leicester."

"Really?" Priya sat up. She had only been trying to distract her friend, now she was interested too.

"A monk at Leicester Abbey, called Henry Knighton, wrote after the Black Death in the 14th century how the sheep died and their bodies were so corrupted by the plague that no animal or bird would touch them. Sheep and cattle who survived wandered through the crops since there was no one to harvest the fields or look after the animals. He wrote that no such universal or horrifying mortality had taken place within living memory." Rita told her.

"It must have been terrifying." Priya sympathised.

"The death toll was between a third and a quarter of the population." Rita nodded. "The City only recovered as quickly as it did because people moved here from other places. It was a prosperous agricultural centre and trade and industry grew around it."

"Quarantine is still an important way of restricting an epidemic." Priya said, going back to what happened in Venice. "Of course, nowadays we would send people in decontamination suits" she added, "Like for the Ebola outbreaks. Those suits look well scary!"

Rita was nodding. "The Venetians who dealt with plague victims had an outfit too." she told her friend." You probably don't realise it, but the masks used in Venice for the plague still appear in the Carnevale processions."

"You went to the Carnival this year, didn't you?" Priya asked, then wished she hadn't as it might upset her friend to think about Matteo, just what she was trying to distract her from. But Rita was thinking about her favourite subject, history, not her personal life, and did not seem to notice.

"Yes," she replied, "It was amazing! Cold, because this was in February, but very lively with lots of people in costumes. Balloons and masks were everywhere. It was such a great thing to go to in the middle of winter. It was so colourful and exciting!"

Rita went silent for a minute, thinking that had been the time she had felt closest to Matteo. It had been great to be reunited at the end of February after weeks apart, and it was lucky that she could stay with Matteo in the trattoria as accommodation in the city was scarce, the Carnevale being one of the most well-known events in the world. People flocked there to fill the narrow streets and bridges. They had sat close together to watch firework displays and gone on a ghost tour and a food tour, even though Matteo said they were a way of ripping off tourists.

Rita returned to her train of thought, "The bird-like masks that are worn in the Carnival represent the masks worn by the plague doctors, 'medico della peste' they were called." she told her friend. "The masks were made of leather and made to hold fragrances to ward off illness. The plague doctors would be covered head to foot in dark clothes made of wax-coated canvas to protect them from the illness."

"I would be scared if one them visited me" Priya said, recalling the masks, which were white with a large beak, making the wearer unrecognisable. "I guess the costumes gave them some protection."

"People sought spiritual protection, too, and still do." Rita told her. "In the 17th century the Doge, the ruler of Venice, built a church as an offering for the city's deliverance from the plague. It is the Basilica Santa Maria della Salute which basically means Basilica of Saint Mary of Health and is a very distinctive part of the Venetian skyline. On November 22 every year there is a procession to it. We saw it, Matteo and me. They build a pontoon – a sort of temporary bridge resting on barges-to cross the Grand Canal from St Mark's Square. Venetians flock to it to give thanks for their deliverance from the plague and the canal is completely congested. There's lots of excitement and they let off balloons over the canal. I've been inside the church. It is not so very different from a temple, really, it has two domes and two bell towers, all highly decorated, and is filled inside and out with statues. People leave flowers there, just like we do. Everything in it relates to the Black Death."

"I s'pose they thought they could bring themselves better luck," Priya shook her head, "Since they thought the plague was a punishment. To get them back for their sins." she said.

"'Spect so." Rita replied, sounding distracted.

Priya noticed that Rita was not looking at her screen any more. Out of her vision, Rita was searching the possessions she had brought back from Leamington. There among the pile of books was her copy of the Divine Comedy. Priya's mention of sin had reminded her of Dante's interest in the Arsenal and his description of boiling oil to punish certain sinners. The book, the police officers had told her, could well have acted as a signal to someone at the trattoria, either of itself or because there was a coded message inside it. Would this book help the police, she wondered? She thought probably not, as she had not noticed anything unusual about it, although it was always possible a message had been left on a piece of paper inside the book, which had been removed when she arrived. After all, she would hardly have read the whole book on the way over from Leamington. Still, it was worth a try; the police might find something to help them. Sliding the book from the pile, a bookmark fell out of it onto the floor. Rita picked it up. It was the business card given to her by Olga Kelenko, the one she had taken a picture of for DCI Bridge. She had forgotten that was where she had put it.

"What are you looking at?" Priya called out.

"Mmmn. I wonder." Rita said out loud. "Oh, sorry." she added, finally looking back at the screen again. "Something just struck me. OK if I make a call?"

"Sure" Priya shrugged, glad to see her friend's enthusiasm was returning, although enthusiasm for what she did not know.

Chapter

10

"Venice, its temples and palaces did seem like fabrics of enchantment piled to heaven."

Percy Bysse Shelley

Monday 26th June 2017 11am

Rita was standing on a step. She was looking at the pealing paint on the front door of a terraced house in Ashby de la Zouch, failing to find either a bell which worked or a door knocker. She opted for banging on the door, since there seemed to be no other means of summoning the occupants, and hoped someone had heard her. The town was twinned with the French town of Pithiviers, she had read on a sign on her drive over there from Leicester. The house was in a road just off the broad main thoroughfare of Market Street. There she had glimpsed several Elizabethan half-timbered houses and bow fronted shops whose premises dated from Georgian times. The town, she knew, was called Ashby in the Domesday book and the French addition was added by the La Zouch family when they acquired the estate. Names changed through time, Rita knew. Royal Leamington Spa, as it was properly titled, had been referred to as 'Lamintone' in the Domesday Book of 1081, and was later known as Leamington Priors, until the medicinal benefits of the waters attracted the attention of Queen Victoria, who first visited the town as a princess in 1830 and returned as Queen in 1858. It was she who bestowed the 'Royal' title on the growing town, hence her statue, which Rita had often passed, on The Parade outside the Town Hall.

Industry had come to Ashby in the nineteenth century in

the form of a number of coal mines which developed around the town, as well as brick-making businesses. The house Rita was looking at was in a row dating from this Victorian expansion. Each of the houses had a wooden front door inside a brick arch and beside it a bow window. On the floor above, two narrow windows provided light to the bedrooms. A large chimney on the roof demonstrated what had been the main source of heat in the past. This was practical housing, probably made with local bricks, for workers and their families, Rita thought.

A woman, whose age Rita found hard to guess, opened the door just as she was thinking of knocking again. The woman was about 5 feet tall and probably a candidate for type 2 diabetes, judging by her waistline, or lack of it. She had ostentatiously dyed black hair in a knot at the back of her head and over-bright red lipstick somewhere in the region of her mouth. She held a mug of something aloft in her hand, to show she had been disturbed.

"He's upstairs" was all she said, and gestured with her free hand to the staircase behind her. Rita thanked her and passed through the hall, noticing the thick tartan patterned curtain that was hanging at the door to keep out draughts. Rita progressed upwards as directed. The woman went back to whatever daytime TV she was watching. It sounded like Murder She Wrote, Jessica Fletcher on the trail again, or maybe it was an old Miss Marple. Rita's housemates had flicked through these programmes when they were bored during the day between lectures.

Simon was in a small bedroom at the front of the house. Just like the one Rita had occupied in Leamington. She found the room by following the sound of a printer which, together with three screens which were flashing different images, almost filled the room. A couple of lap tops were also active. It was like being in PC World at Fosse Park, a shop at the retail park in Leicester where her brother, Nayan, liked to hang out. Simon was hunched over a screen, sitting on a black office chair on wheels which he demonstrated before Rita could speak by gliding from one screen to another and back again without his feet touching the floor.

"Impressive" Rita said. Simon looked up, pushing his large grey earphones from his head to rest round his neck.

"Thanks for agreeing to help me." she said.

"If I can" he answered, and pointed to the green picnic chair which was folded and propped up against the wall behind the door. She gathered it, set it up and sat close to him. While she did this, Simon continued to watch the various screens, typing in commands every so often.

Rita had time to look at Simon carefully. He had put on weight since the first time they had met, which was when he came to stay at Athena's bed and breakfast following the unfortunate death of his father. Too much computer time and take-away food she surmised. An aunt, the person who had answered the door, was putting him up for the time being, begrudgingly, she had gathered from the brief phone call she had made to Simon and the cold welcome she had received when she arrived at the house. Simon was roughly the same age as Rita, although that was hard to realise. He looked younger, in loose-fitting grey track suit bottoms and a baggy pale pink T-shirt. His mousy coloured hair was long and wavy and could benefit from a wash, she thought.

"You said there might be a way to get into an iPhone, the information on it, that is? The woman who it belonged to was murdered, as I told you, and the police can't get Apple to help." Rita tried to explain the problem again.

Simon did not seem to be paying attention, his eyes on a screen, his fingers dancing over a key board. "I don't need the details " he said, not stopping any of these activities. "Did she have the app?"

"What app?" Rita asked.

"The one to upload to online. You create your own

archive." Simon told her, "That would make it easy for us. But we'd need her passcode. Then we could get into her contact list, messages, photos."

"Oh dear," Rita said, sighing with disappointment and sinking a little in the picnic chair. "I don't know it." her head was hanging down. Had she come to Ashby on a wild goose chase?

Simon was talking again as if she had not spoken. "The word is that in the States a company is developing a Graykey, a box that can unlock an iPhone. I dunno what will happen. It might help the feds but it would be expensive and what if it got into the hands of perps? Man, we could do with it now!" Simon chuckled to himself.

"Let's try anyway." he said, showing that he had heard what Rita said. Simon rubbed his hands together enthusiastically, "I like a challenge."

"Can you?" Rita was surprised.

"I've got iRefone which lets us access data iCloud backup files," he told her, tapping some keys until a window opened on his screen requesting the iCloud account and password.

"So, we're stuck?" Rita said, exasperated. "Not yet" Simon replied. "What was her name?" Rita told him again.

"Don't look" Simon told her. Rita peeked anyway, she would not understand enough to tell anyone what he had done. He seemed to be putting Olga's name into another software package. It was producing a list until it narrowed down to three choices.

"OK" Simon spoke again, whether to himself or to Rita was unclear.

"Let's get to work". It took two attempts to get the right one.

"Now we need to guess the password" Simon said, leaning slightly in Rita's direction but not making eye contact, "What do you know about her? Pets? Hobbies?"

"Not much" Rita confessed. She felt into her pocket for

the business card Olga had given her. "I have a few phone numbers and.. oh.." Rita realised there was something written on the back of the card. It was in green ink, so very faint. Perhaps that was why she had not seen it before.

Simon raised his eyebrows in a question.

"Never changing" it says, Rita said, puzzled. "Perhaps she wrote that for a case she was on? It does not make any sense."

Simon shrugged his shoulders, and turned back to his screen. "People always write their passwords down, despite all the warnings." he said, "Maybe it's a motto of something." he suggested, "A football club?"

Rita did not think that was very likely. "We can try it anyway." Simon offered, and did. It did not work.

What Simon had said about mottos was nagging in Rita's head. "Hang on. She studied Classics. What about a Latin or Greek version of that motto?" she was thinking out loud now. "The Leicester motto is Semper Eadem" she told him. "Maybe try that?"

Simon started typing, checking the spelling with Rita. "Gotcha!" he said, grinning.

Monday 26th June 2017 6.45pm

Rita arrived back at Elm Drive just as Nayan was leaving the house. After thanking Simon, and his aunt, who barely acknowledged her departure, and before leaving Ashby, she had taken the opportunity to look at the ruins of the castle which were signed from the main road. She had found them quite atmospheric in their own way, and she sent an Instagram picture to Priya. The castle dated from the fifteenth century and was the work of the first Lord Hastings, Rita discovered by googling the place. Sir Walter Scott was reputed to have used the castle as the setting for a tournament in his book Ivanhoe, and Mary Queen of Scots had been held there for a time. Rita was unable to fully distract herself, however.

Walking around the red brick ruins, which sat in a sea of overgrown grass, and sitting in the Georgian tea shop where she stopped off before driving back, Rita found her mind repeatedly returning to the question of what to do with the information that Simon had unearthed. Now she was almost glad to allow herself to be distracted by her younger brother.

"How's it going?" she asked him.

"Just waiting for the busy time." he told her. She noticed he was wearing his moped gear, helmet in hand, ready to make more deliveries. She had not realised it had got so late. Almost 7pm already.

"I'm doing ok sis." Nayan told Rita, "But I'm really worried about my friend Mo." He confided.

Although excited by the progress she had made with Simon, Rita decided to wait before going into the house. It looked like Nayan needed to talk. His blue Peugeot moped was polished and poised, facing the road. He was ready for action. He had double-checked the storage box at the back to make sure he had plenty of capacity to carry whatever the evening might bring by way of orders. Sometimes it would be just a couple ordering in Indian takeaway. At other times it might be a pizza party, when half a dozen or more pizzas might be ordered, all large size of course, plus garlic bread, and other sides and lots of drinks. That was a challenge on a moped, but one he was willing to try if the tips were good Some customers were very generous, either out of their nature or because they had consumed a lot of alcohol. Others were mean; they just paid for the food online and shut the door in his face once it had been handed over. You could not tell from the outside of the house what sort of reception you would get. He had learnt that. It evened out in the end, and if he wanted to join the police, which was his ultimate ambition, acquiring people skills was a good thing. He was learning to observe different kinds of people and to communicate with them, he thought.

"Why are you concerned about Mo?" asked Rita, it was not like Nayan to worry about his friends. He was usually too consumed with himself, in her opinion. Perhaps her little brother was growing up at last?

"Well, he's been doing this delivery work like me, only he doesn't have a generous family behind him." Nayan told her as they sat side by side, perched on the low brick wall at the end of what had been a garden once – her father's pride and joy- and now was paved to provide parking space for the vehicles of his widow and offspring. "Less maintenance" was how Padma had justified the transition to herself.

"Mmmmn." Rita nodded. She knew that Padma had bought Nayan's moped out of money their father had left. "Against my better judgement" as she said, "Those things are death traps! So dangerous in busy traffic, and you young men go too fast, but I suppose I can't stop you!" and she had thrown up her hands in a gesture of helplessness. The truth was she had not liked him doing deliveries on his bicycle, a large pack strapped to his back so that he had looked like a blue tortoise. She hoped the moped was marginally safer.

"The pay's OK if you get the right trips." Nayan was saying. "Local ones which use up less fuel. The trouble is, there is no guarantee of work- it depends on getting requests from the call centre- so your income fluctuates. Then you've got expenses- fuel, wear and tear on the bike, speeding fines."

"Don't tell Mum about those" Rita advised, "She'll go spare."

"I am careful" Nayan reassured his sister, "But the call centre guys sometimes push you, especially if they are short of staff at busy times, and then there are roadworks which can hold you up. If you need the money you push yourself."

"I get the picture" Rita said, starting to see her brother's part-time work as quite stressful and not the easy money she had thought it to be.

"What is Mo's trouble, then?" she asked, "Is he behind

with his bills?"

"Well, yeh. It started like that." Nayan said, getting up to check out his moped again while he waited for his instructions.

"Then the debts were handed to an enforcement agency" he told her.

"Oh no" said Rita, fearing something bad.

"They sent bailiffs who nearly took his moped but he managed to make an arrangement with them." Nayan told her.

"Phew" said Rita, "Sounds like Mo is having it rough."

"Yes, but that's not what I'm worried about." Nayan sighed, "To make the weekly payments he took a dodgy loan, from a bloke he met while on a delivery. He was obviously a dealer."

"You do mean drugs?" Rita checked. Given her recent experience with the police, Nayan had her full attention now.

Her brother nodded. "The loan had conditions. Mo has to do deliveries for him. Some of them are well dodge. And if he doesn't do as they say there are threats. They are nasty people, Rita."

"Wow" Rita sympathised, "Sounds like.." but her words were cut off as Nayan's phone finally sprang into action. He jumped onto his transport and sped away. Rita went indoors, more ideas racing through her head.

Chapter

11

"In the glare of day, there is little poetry about Venice, but under the charitable moon her stained palaces are white again."

Mark Twain

Tuesday 27th June 2017 2pm

A tense meeting was taking place at Leicester Police HQ in Enderby. Superintendent Forster was demanding answers on the Olga Kelenko murder. There were none to give her. The team were working on theories and lines of inquiry, but there was no evidence to link any particular suspect to the crime.

"Too many cooks.." she was saying under her breath, not bothering to finish the saying, while she examined her nails, which had been freshly done at the nail salon that morning, and listened to Detective Sergeant McKenzie's summary of what fell under the heading of 'progress' on their agenda, although it was looking like a misnomer.

The DS had just gone through a list of different units within the police force who were involved with the case; EMSOU, Leicestershire Police, Essex Police, Brentwood and Epping Forest Community Policing Team, Warwickshire Police and their neighbourhood policing team and the NCA. That was the point at which Sue Forster had muttered, "Let's not forget the Garde" before adding the start of the epithet about people who spoil the broth. Criminals were not respecting the lines between police forces; never had cooperation and information sharing been so important.

Olga Kelenko had died hours before being found, according to the pathologist. The cause of death was drowning. The water definitely came from the Severn and Trent company, tests had shown.

"We have a crime committed locally but no crime scene." DCI Bridge tried to come to his Detective Sergeant's rescue, seeing the discontent on his boss's face. "We put the victim's details out on social media and in the local rag, once we had the information from Rita Patel…"

"Oh yes, Rita Patel," the Superintendent tightened her pony tail as she sat straighter in her chair. She had come across the young woman when she was reported missing not long ago. Rita was not one to keep out of hot water, it seemed. "Who smuggled drugs into the country on more than one occasion?" Sue Forster showed she was up to speed.

"Yeh, but with the knowledge of the NCA and Customs," DS Brett McKenzie put in a plea of mitigation for Rita, who had cooperated fully with DCs Fryer and Singh as far as he could tell from the latter's detailed report.

"But, despite surveillance, the NCA weren't able to name any of the people in the drug smuggling ring?" Sue Forster sighed. A lot of working hours had been spent on this investigation, but with no tangible results. In police dramas, CCTV footage or DNA material generally turned up by the last fifteen minutes at least so the case could be wrapped up. If only real life was so simple, she thought, looking at the time on her phone. She could only spare about twenty minutes for this briefing before she went to a meeting of top brass to discuss an extension of on-line crime reporting. The answer to reduced numbers of officers was digital, it seemed, even if computers could not tackle knife- wielding, gun-toting, fist-throwing criminals, or stop a robbery in progress.

"Of the people we do know about, where were they when she was killed?" she asked.

"Well, Ryan Aldred, the ex-boyfriend, was in Essex, his alibi checks out." Detective Sergeant McKenzie told her.

"And Rita Patel? Where was she?" the Superintendent

asked, looking at a message coming through on her phone about another matter.

"At university near Coventry" the DCI put in, not choosing to argue about whether Rita was capable of inflicting such horrible suffering on another human being, "Again, her movements are supported by witnesses."

"And we think the drug angle is the strongest? That our victim was investigating the finances of the businesses her clients had invested in and hit on a drug cartel?"

Jamie Bridge and Brett McKenzie nodded.

"We don't think there's anything in the Ukrainian angle? I understand Intelligence suggested her father might have been bumped off by Russian agents because of his involvement in the move to Ukrainian independence?"

Jamie Bridge and Brett McKenzie shook their heads.

"There's nothing to suggest that Olga Kelenko was investigating anything which might have threatened the Russian state." the DCI told her, "Of course, we are still waiting on Apple to give us full access to the information on her iPhone, but you can't really imagine that Russian agents would attack a person here, in Leicestershire, in broad daylight?"

"I agree it's a long shot." the Superintendent conceded, checking the time again. "Let's give it another week." she said, "If there is no new information and there are no new lines of inquiry then you need to shut it down and move on." she directed, shaking her head regretfully. It looked like the case would remain unsolved. Chalk another one up to the drug gangs, she thought.

Tuesday 27th June 2017 9pm

Richard III was holding his crown in the air, as usual, while Rita stood beside his statue in what the City of Leicester was now calling its Cultural Quarter. The King stood proud, keeping an eye on his tomb in the Cathedral to one side of him and his Visitor Centre, which encapsulated the spot where his body had been found, on the other. The Centre displayed information which Leicester University had discovered about the manner of his death and of the deformity which he was alleged, in Tudor times, to have had. Disability was little understood in Elizabethan times and often seen as a sign of moral impairment, Rita knew. It was Thomas More who had written that Richard was short in height and crook-backed, his left shoulder much higher than his right. The skeleton in the car park had been found to suffer some scoliosis, but not as pronounced as More had stated. Rita looked up at Richard, who was not at all deformed in his statue form, then scanned the street for signs of Morwenna and her boyfriend, who had said they would meet her there.

"Cool. Sweet. See you then." back in Leicester after a few days in the Caribbean, Morwenna had sounded keen to meet up, provided Rita would come with them to the bar where she and Toby would be hanging out that evening.

"Have you seen my Mum, she said you had. She's in such a state over my Dad leaving, I've been really worrying about her.."

Not worried enough to stop you going to the Caribbean, Rita had thought, but she said nothing, not least because Morwenna was still speaking.

"I don't see the problem, they've both got their own lives and I'm off their hands now I'm leaving uni and starting work. She's moving to Devon, you know, did she tell you that? I'm not sure it's a good idea. It's a nice part of the world, I went to Totnes when I was at Exeter uni, but I wouldn't want to live there! Not enough going on, no clubs or good bars to speak of. And what if she doesn't like it?"

Morwenna paused to take a breath at last and Rita took the opportunity to interject.

"It's OK Morwenna. Chill." she tried to calm her friend,

"Athena seemed very together to me and ready to move on. She'll have room for guests so maybe we can visit her together some time? We can make plans when we are living in the flat?" Rita had brought the subject round to the reason she wanted to see Morwenna. There were details to be filled in about the flat share.

Rita had rushed back from her yoga class in order to be at their rendezvous point on time. She was getting into yoga now and happy to drop into classes when she could find them, whether in Leamington or Leicester. It was definitely contributing to her flexibility, which she needed to keep up with Nayan and his mad ideas like skydiving, and she found it relaxing, especially the sessions when they meditated for a while. It helped her to focus on what was important and to tune out things which were just annoying. She needed to keep in that mindset, she told herself as she shifted her weight from foot to foot and checked her phone in case Morwenna had sent an apologetic message. Like there was any chance of that! Meeting up with Morwenna might test her new serenity she thought.

Tuesday 27th June 2017 9.30pm

In the bar at last, Rita, wearing a loose-fitting black dress with small sprigs of blue flowers on the dark background, found herself stepping sideways to her right in her bright blue court shoes and leaning her head nearer to Morwenna's to hear what her friend was trying to communicate to her. The wine bar, Veenos, not far from Market Place, specialised in Italian wines. Was there no getting away from memories of her time abroad? Rita had thought as she entered.

The interior was dark, with a few coloured lights moving around the customers so that occasionally, out of the gloom, like a modern art installation, a face would be garishly lit for a few seconds, in a haze of green, blue or yellow. The effect was not unlike the way colours flew through the air during the Holi spring celebrations, which Rita had managed to catch at Spinney Hill Park in the city in March. She had travelled to Leicester by train so she could sleep, on the way, her head resting on the table in front of her seat. She had been finding it hard to fit in her studies, her visits to Venice, and the expectations of her mother. "You were not here for Diwali" her mother had reproached her, "You can't let me down over Holi as well!" Padma, Rita knew, was keen to have all her children present, since her sister, Jaina would have her twin daughters in attendance.

Rita blinked hard. It was as if by thinking about the fun at Holi, when she had last been with her cousins, she had somehow conjured them up. No, there they actually were, her twin cousins sitting across a table from one another, cradling glasses of wine and picking at a sharing board of food. One of the twins, Shona, or was it Shreya, was deep in conversation with a boy of about her own age who was sitting next to her. As Rita watched with fascination, an older man, probably in his late twenties, wearing a brown leather jacket, came to their table bearing more drinks on a tray. He put the tray on the table before seating himself beside the other twin, patting her on the thigh in greeting. Not a casual acquaintance, then, Rita thought, and started doing some calculations. The twins must be 18 years old; did she vaguely remember her mother mentioning this in one of her telephone conversations? She really should pay more attention when her mother was speaking, Rita thought. Didn't she say that her cousins' parents had booked them a party at Revolution, another bar in town, on New Walk? It had sounded a bit over the top to Rita, but nothing was good enough for the daughters of Jaina and Bandhu, as her mother was always reminding her. They had saved to put the girls through private school, and now were hoping to reap the rewards with good university places for them both.

Educational skills were not the only ones they had picked up, apparently, judging by the assurance with which her cousins were enjoying themselves that evening. Shouldn't they be revising for their A levels? Rita thought. Instead, they had clearly spent some time getting ready to go out- both seemed to be wearing a lot of make-up and their hair had been styled into ringlets. They looked like they had been in the bar for a while judging by the empty glasses on the table. Rita wondered how much their mother, her aunt Jaina, knew about this. She was just deciding whether to let the girls know she was here when another thought struck her. It was difficult to recognise faces in the strange strobing light of the bar, but there was something familiar about the man in the leather jacket. Before she could formulate the idea that was just occurring to her, Morwenna spoke in Rita's ear.

"Justin's been like so attentive… we've hardly had a chance to speak to him." Morwenna was reproaching Rita, "Back to the flat after the next one?" Morwenna, wearing a green jumpsuit, towered over Rita in her designer heels as she made this suggestion. It was several cocktails since they had entered the establishment, so she was relieved they might be leaving soon. On the other hand, there would be the problem of Justin, Toby's friend, who was standing to her left.

"I'm not sure that Justin..." Rita began tentatively.

"Yeh, yeh" said Morwenna nodding as she misunderstood what Rita was trying to say, "You can talk to Justin some more when we leave. Get to know him better." That was what Rita was afraid of.

The meeting had clearly been a set-up. She had realised this when Morwenna finally turned up at the Richard III statue with not one, but two, men in tow. Rita had wanted to talk to Morwenna about the arrangements for the flat share – keys, rent, bills, that sort of thing- and to see the room she would be using. Morwenna and Toby obviously had another agenda – setting up Rita and Justin to meet each other. "He's single, like yourself." Morwenna had said pointedly when she made the introductions.

Rita had spent most of the evening sipping at cranberry juice and lemonade and smiling politely as Justin told her about his job as a trainee accountant, his flat share, on Colton Street, near Leicester University and within walking distance of the town centre, apparently, the rugby team he played for at weekends, and how he and Toby had been great mates since school. Justin was also an expert on Brexit, unfortunately, and willing to offer the Prime Minister, Theresa May, advice should she ask. "She should never have issued the article 50 notice in February" according to him. "She should have listened to the ambassador, the one who resigned, Sir Ivan Rogers." he went on. "She should not have called that General Election, what an own goal!" As Rita listened, she thought perhaps her practice with her mother had not been wasted, she knew how to appear interested while thinking of something else.

The issue that was buzzing inside Rita's head, and would not go away, like a bluebottle trapped in a room, was the identity of the man drinking with her cousins. She had only seen him a few times, one being his wedding, when he had been dressed very differently and looking nervous, not relaxed and laughing as he was today. She had also seen him not long after the birth of his son, when, again, he had been tense and preoccupied, trying to cope with the responsibility of a wife who had just given birth and a new-born son, Theeran. This was Jai, Meera's husband, she was sure of it. Rita's heart suddenly felt heavy. Should she speak to anyone about this? And if so, who?

Chapter

12

"General Grant seriously remarked to a particularly bright young woman that Venice would be a fine City if it were drained."

Henry Adams

Tuesday 27th June 2017 11pm

Justin was pressing on, oblivious to Rita's lack of interest, including in his criticisms the former Prime Minister, David Cameron, for holding the referendum, Boris Johnson for supporting Leave, and the Russian government for interfering and spreading 'fake news'. Rita was trying not to look in the twins' direction. Embarrassing as this was, it would be worse if they knew she had seen them, wouldn't it? Never mind for Jai. What would she say? Rita tried to adjust her face in order to look interested in what Justin was talking about and transferred her weight from foot to foot, swilling the ice at the bottom of her glass of cranberry juice to give her something to focus on. Thanks to the increased noise in the bar Rita could hear only snatches, anyway, to which she nodded politely. ".... Democratic and Unionist Party, ... Supreme Court ....meaningful vote ......"

Rita was not sure whether the alcohol was making Justin so loquacious or whether he was like this all the time. "No wonder Kenneth Clarke said she was a 'difficult woman'" Justin was carrying on, "She does not seem to grasp the realities."

"What about...?" Rita started, thinking she might as well get Justin's take on the Labour party under Jeremy Corbyn. Did he think they would do a better job? But Justin was not interested in listening, it seemed, and steamed on. "Really, we should just start again." he was saying, "Stop the clock on the article 50 notice and have another referendum. I think people are beginning to see that what the Leave leaders were telling them wasn't the true picture, those figures for the NHS on the side of the bus, for example, or those trade deals which we were told it would be so easy to negotiate."

"Could we do that?" Rita was asking out of politeness when Morwenna, finally, made her announcement that it was time to leave. Rita was relieved to find her incipient headache disappeared when the cool evening air hit her face. She was not sickening for something, then, it was just being with Justin plus, she had to admit to herself, an uneasy feeling about one of the twins, she still could not be sure which, and Jai. Putting that situation to the back of her mind, as they headed for a taxi to take them to the flat, on Watkin Road in Freemans Meadow, near the Kingpower Stadium, Rita was dreading being entertained by more of Justin's political views. She pulled her turquoise pashmina closer round her shoulders, her black bag with the elephant motif in sequins, which she had bought at Leicester market, swinging from her shoulder on its slender shiny strap.

Morwenna and Toby were ahead of them, ambling arm in arm. The space between Justin and Rita on the pavement was filled with awkwardness as they walked behind their friends "Have you been abroad very much?" Rita tried before Justin could get back to telling her where the government had gone wrong. Rita thought a man of such strong opinions on international politics must have travelled widely. She had only been to a few places in India, on trips with her family, and in Europe, including her time in Italy. Justin's experience, however, seemed confined to package holidays in destinations well-known for all the wrong reasons. He embarked on a story about what he and Toby got up to in Ibiza. Rita was nodding and trying to laugh in the right places, while thinking that, if Morwenna was going to continue to try to set her up on dates like this when they shared the flat, it was going to be a very tricky time. They had reached the taxi queue and the embarrassment of Justin and Rita became more acute as the couples either side of them got to grips with one another's bodies and tongues. Meanwhile Toby, using his Bluetooth ear piece, was ordering pizza – "Vegetarian for you, Rita?" he asked her, "What's the address again, babe?" he checked with Morwenna, and stroked her bare arms while he confirmed the order.

Rita stared at the road and willed the queue to move. She got her wish. Several taxis appeared at once and they climbed into the third. It was a black cab, like a London taxi. Morwenna took the middle of the back seat, with Rita and Toby either side of her. Justin sat on the folding seat opposite Rita and travelled backwards. His anecdotes had switched to stag parties; there was a bridegroom he had left in his boxer shorts tied to a lamppost in Norfolk and there were various cities in Europe where he and his friends had, according to him, caned it and had terrorised the local population with their drunken behaviour, Krakow and Riga being two of them, although Justin had ended up too drunk or ill to recall much of it.

Rita nodded while she looked out of the cab window at the dark sky and the yellow street lights. She thought back to Venice. It was thankfully not high on the list for stag and hen parties. She could not imagine how awful it would be to be trapped on those bridges and narrow passages by large groups of raucous drunk people in fancy dress. The taxi was starting to move slowly, caught up in late night traffic. A scene was being played out on Belvoir Street as they drove along it. At first Rita thought perhaps she was projecting, based on Justin's anecdotes of inebriation, but no, this was real. A man seemed to stagger and collapse while his companion was taking the opportunity to vomit in the gutter. It was like a scene from a Hogarth picture, she was thinking, when, the next second, Rita recognised the individuals involved. The two women were her twin cousins, the vomiting man was Jai, and the collapsed man was their other companion. Rita's jaw fell in horror as the taxi finally picked up speed.

Wednesday 28ᵗʰ June 2017 12.15 am

It was getting late, or early in the morning, depending on your point of view. Arriving at the flat, Toby had paid the taxi driver using his phone, Morwenna had brandished the key fob to gain entry to the building and the four of them had taken a ride in the lift to the second floor. Once inside, Justin made for the en suite in Morwenna's part of the flat, while Toby headed for the sofa in the middle of the living room and took control of the remote, scrolling through the large TV screen on the wall for films to watch on Netflix.

"Yours is the room at the front." Morwenna had told Rita, waving down the corridor which linked the rooms. Rita wandered along and called into the bathroom first, this would be her sole preserve as Morwenna had her own facilities. It was lit with spotlights and had the latest kind of shower with complicated-looking taps. The tiles were in a soft green colour. It would be fine, she thought. Morwenna's bathroom was next door, she sensed, as, through the thin walls, she could hear Toby on the phone. As she was wondering why he needed to make a call in private, Rita realised she could actually hear most of it as he was too drunk to talk quietly. He seemed to be ordering something and negotiating a price.

The bedroom, she was pleased to note, was a decent size, with a double bed, wardrobe and small table by the bed, all white and from IKEA, probably the work of Athena, Rita guessed. The room looked out in the direction of the stadium, where Leicester City play, which made for an interesting view but might make it noisy on match days, she thought. The proximity would probably make her popular with her brothers, which was a mixed blessing. The gold shiny curtains in the room were not to Rita's taste but she could bring her own, she decided. Maybe she could get some to match her elephant cushions perhaps, she was thinking, when another thought struck her. Had the police monitored all the items she had brought into the country which might have been filled with drugs, she wondered? She must check the cushions when she got home.

Back in the kitchen area, which was at one end of the living room, a clinical affair in white with integral appliances and a tap that dispensed hot water, Rita made herself a mint tea, using a bag she had brought with her, while Morwenna raided the fridge for craft beer and Chardonnay. Straightening up and handing over the bottles, Morwenna sent her bank details for the rent payments to Rita's phone.

"First of the month, yeh? Starting in August? This is going to be soo great!" she said excitedly, then, "Bring the corn chips, will you?" Morwenna pointed to a bag on the cupboard next to the fridge. With the last unused fingers on her left hand, Rita obliged.

They all settled in the living room area, divided from the kitchen by a glass dining table and with brown high-backed chairs. Toby and Justin had agreed on a box set, something American with gangsters being infiltrated by FBI officers who quickly seemed to behave worse than the gang members themselves. The beer bottles and the Chardonnay were placed on the white IKEA coffee table, and the corn chips were passed around in their bag. Toby had flopped on the brown leather sofa and indicated that Morwenna should join him. Rita took the white IKEA chair and Justin sat on a brown bean bag on the beige carpeted floor. He did not seem to mind.

It was just at the end of the first episode, with the blood-soaked body of one of the FBI agents floating in a swimming pool, that the intercom to the flat buzzed. Everyone jumped, then they laughed at themselves. Toby sprang up to answer.

"At last!" he said, pausing the film.

Half a minute later, Toby was opening the door, displaying more energy than he had for most of the evening so far. Rita followed him and caught sight of the delivery person over Toby's shoulder.

"Mo!" Rita said, recognising Nayan's friend immediately, even though he was still wearing his helmet and had his face partly obscured by pizza boxes.

"Hi Rita" he acknowledged her sheepishly. "The meat feast and the special are for you" he addressed Toby, as he handed over the boxes to him.

"Thanks man." Toby said and gave him some notes out of his jeans pocket. "Can you pay him the rest?" he asked Rita as he headed first to Morwenna's room and then back to the living area with the food. Mo told Rita what was owed, which seemed to be most of it, and she pulled some notes from her bag, which she had left in the hallway, giving Mo a generous tip. "Thanks" he said hoarsely and was gone. Rita shut the door and joined the others.

Wednesday 28th June 2017 2am

Rita let herself into 10 Elm Drive as quietly as she could. She had parked her car at Morwenna's before catching a bus into town for their meeting, so she was able to drive herself home. She had left Morwenna and Toby the worse for wear. She suspected that more than alcohol had been consumed, given the hyped-up way they were both behaving, but it was none of her business. Fortunately, Justin was one of those people who fall asleep when they have drunk too much. Before she left, they had laid him out on the sofa with a blanket. The box set had proved a bit confusing – the drama kept shifting from the present to the past, and they found themselves discussing it more than they were watching it. Perhaps she would watch it again some time and see if it made more sense, or she could look on Twitter to find out what others made of it. Meanwhile, before she turned in for the night, she needed to check something. Taking off her blue shoes, Rita crept into the living room and put on the light. She was not prepared for what she saw. Rita let out a gasp. The room was empty. There was no furniture in it at all.

Chapter

13

"Venice was and is full of lost places where people put up for sale the last worn bits of their souls, hoping no one will buy."

Ray Bradbury

Wednesday 28th June 2017 7.30 am

"If you listened or spent more time at home" Padma was saying as she chewed her muesli, "You would know what has happened. The living room is going to be decorated -today- and the furniture is in store."

Padma rose from the table to make herself some tea. The Breakfast Show was on the kitchen TV with the sound turned down. Rita's eyes were too blurred from lack of sleep to read the words scurrying across the bottom of the screen. Some video footage of the Queen in a smart blue suit appeared; at least Rita could recognise her.

"You see, the Queen went to Grenfell yesterday" her mother was saying as she took her green tea back to her place at the table," She knows what to do in a crisis, unlike those politicians!" Padma shook her head. "I can't bear to think of those poor people not able to get out of the building in time, it makes me shudder." Padma did indeed seem to shiver in her dark blue silk dressing gown. "And those who survived have lost everything, everything! So really it is a small thing that we have had our living room possessions put away for a few days." she continued as she chased the last of the dried fruit and grains around her bowl with her spoon.

Rita, who had had about three hours sleep, was trying to take this in. She had been so afraid that they had been burgled and, because of what she was looking for, she feared the burglary might be her fault. Had the gang been trying to retrieve more drugs?

"Remind me what you are having done" she said to placate her mother.

"Shona and Shreya will be here at 10" her mother said, "They are earning extra cash now their A levels are done. They've done an on-line course on how to do decorating and they are coming to give the room a fresh look."

Rita thought back to the night before. What her mother had said explained why her cousins had not been at home revising. Then she recalled the scene she had witnessed from the taxi, which suggested her cousins and their companions had been drinking heavily. Had they made it home safely? Would the twins be in any state to take on this task today, she wondered?

"Just painting or wall paper too?" she asked tremulously.

"Oh, just paint" her mother replied, to her relief. Perhaps they could just about manage that, Rita thought.

"Bandhu, their father, has let them borrow his ladders. The colour I've chosen is on the counter." Padma indicated the pile of papers she kept in the corner of the kitchen. "Shona and Shreya have a key so they can let themselves in."

Padma crossed the kitchen to add her bowl, spoon and mug to the contents of the dishwasher before inserting a washing tablet in the appropriate compartment, selecting a cleaning cycle, and closing the door with a satisfying click which set the machine purring in motion.

"Now, I have to get to work" Padma said before Rita could ask any more questions, such as, where was the furniture and when would it be coming back? "Empty the dish washer when it finishes will you?" were Padma's last words as she headed upstairs to prepare for a day at the surgery.

Rita rubbed her eyes, which were dry with lack of sleep. Glancing up at the TV screen, Rita saw that the Queen was visiting Grenfell again. The TV companies had so many reporters at the site now that every event had to be examined over and over in minute detail. Pity no one had been there to do that before the fire, Rita reflected, then it might not have happened.

Good luck to her cousins doing a day's decorating if they felt as bad as she did, she thought, and from what she had seen they were probably feeling a whole lot worse. She strolled to the papers on the counter where the colour chart was uppermost. Mid- stone, that was her mother's radical idea for her makeover. Rita was about to move to the dishwasher, to see how long the cycle would take, when she noticed something else in the pile of papers. It was an invoice from a storage company. As she disturbed the pile, a key fell out with the number of a storage room attached to it. All she needed now was a means to get into the building, she thought. Turning over the invoice, she saw her mother had obligingly written four numbers on it - the access code.

"Have a good day!" Padma called from the front door as she left.

"I will, you too." Rita called back, thinking that the dishwasher could wait, she had to get to that storage facility ASAP.

* * *

"What are we doing here, sis?" Mohal wanted to know. He had been in his latest car, a red two-seater Mazda Sport Convertible, waiting for her when she arrived at the Abbey Park car park off Abbey Park Road, close to where the storage place was located. She had known his car would not be suitable for what she had in mind. It was too conspicuous and lacked luggage space. He walked over to her blue Toyota and got in the passenger side.

"I may need some help." Rita said. "If the furniture is

heavy and I can't find what I'm looking for."

"Mum's furniture, you mean?" Mohal was mystified, and worried, "She'll go mad!"

"Not if she doesn't know." was Rita's reply.

"So how are you going to get in?" Mohal asked, "And how do you know exactly where her stuff is?"

In answer, Rita held up the paperwork and the key to show him. "Come on" she said.

Rita had not wanted to involve Mohal. The fewer people implicated in this business the better, she thought, especially when you considered how it turned out for Olga Kelenko. It was because of Olga that she was doing this. She must remember that. If she could find the cushion it might help towards finding some of the people responsible for her death.

Rita used one of the parking spaces at the back reserved for customers and led Mohal confidently to the front of the building, which windows framed in blue paint and glass doors at the entrance. Empty storage boxes could be seen displayed in the foyer with a poster on the wall opposite indicating the prices for purchasing them. There was no sign of anyone in the reception area, but Rita was not phased. She glanced at the note her mother had made, took a deep breath and tried the numbers on the pad by the main door. There was a buzzing sound and she was able to push the door open. They were in.

"Take a trolley!" Rita directed her brother.

"Why?" Mohal was puzzled, "We're not going to take out anything heavy, are we?"

Rita looked up at the ceiling for a second and took a breath. How come her brother was a journalist when he knew so little about how to conduct an investigation? "It will make us blend in, silly." she told him, "No one will question us if we look like we are moving something in or out."

"Oh, all right." Mohal got the picture and fetched a trolley from the collection by the wall. Together they set off, following the directions to unit 238, past rows of identical blue doors. The place was like a labyrinth, Rita thought, and she hoped they would find their way out again. She was glad she had brought company, even if it was only her older brother. She would not feel so confident if she were here by herself. Who knew who you might meet as you went around each corner? What if the gang knew what she was trying to retrieve? What if they had bribed the receptionist, or worse? What if… No, it was better not to speculate. After all, Rita herself had not known what she was going to do until that morning, let alone Mohal, so how could anyone else have anticipated this venture? Keep calm and carry on she told herself.

Rounding yet another corner, Rita and her brother could see that 238 was three doors away. Rita strode up to it, Mohal following with the trolley. Rita put the key in the lock. It would not turn. All this effort for nothing she thought.

"Here, let me." Mohal stepped forward, determined not to be thwarted now they had come this far. Reluctantly, Rita handed over the key.

"Maybe you turned it the wrong way." Mohal said annoyingly, trying the key himself. They both heard it click. At least they could get to look at her mother's furniture, thought Rita, relieved.

The light inside was operated by a white cord which you couldn't really miss as you opened the door. This was just as well, Rita realised, as the sight that met them when the light went on was chaotic. The firm who had moved the furniture would not get prizes for presentation Rita thought. Her mother's three-piece suite was nearest the door, the small tables and the footstool were farthest away. It looked as though they had loaded their van with the lighter things first and unloaded in reverse. Rita had to concede that probably made sense. It meant that when the furniture was loaded back in the van it would be loaded with the heavy items first followed by the lighter and the reverse process would apply when it all went back in the living room. Meanwhile, where was the cushion? Rita scoured the box which the storage unit formed. Just as she caught sight of the cushion, the distinctive yellow fabric making it stand out, Rita could hear footsteps. The geography of the place made it impossible to guess where the sound was coming from.

"OK sis?" Mohal asked. "Seen what you want yet?"

"Sshh!" Rita admonished, putting her finger to her lips as a security guard, wearing a blue shirt and black trousers, appeared to their right. He had a jaunty, confident, way of walking and he rolled his big shoulders as he came towards them.

"Everything all right I hope?" he said, "I'll be in reception if you need anything. Bigger trolley.." he said this as he glanced at the trolley which Mohal had picked out. It was the smallest one. "Or anything."

"Thanks" Rita said. "We should be fine." Mohal nodded in agreement.

"See you later then." the guard said in a friendly manner, and sauntered away down the corridor.

"Phew!" whispered Rita when he was out of earshot. "It's over in that corner, the yellow cushion, can you climb over to get it?"

"We came all the way here and did all this for a cushion?" Mohal said, disgusted. He had given up a game of badminton for this, something he had taken up since he had started going to the gym. He particularly enjoyed playing mixed doubles.

"You'll see." hissed Rita, "Just get it!" she insisted.

"OK" her brother accepted the challenge, "but only if you film me." He handed his phone to his sister.

"Film you?" Rita queried, surprised, "Why?"

"In case I can use it on my vlog of course." Mohal replied.

"Excuse me?" Rita was confused.

"The vlog I've started. It's the new medium. The days of newspapers like the one I work on are numbered, the future is the internet. I want to get a following." He explained as he assessed the furniture like a climber examining a rock face.

"OK" Rita shrugged, willing to placate him, "But don't post it yet or Mum will go ballistic!"

"Oh, she won't see it!" Mohal was dismissive of Rita's fears of being found out, "She can barely send an email." he chuckled.

Sizing up the task, Mohal was glad he was dressed for the gym, in T-shirt, track suit bottoms and trainers. This looked physically challenging. He climbed over the back of the sofa onto the seat, then did the same with one of the chairs, reaching the area where the tables were stored and, by leaning on a table, he was able to stretch out his arm and pick up the cushion by one of its corners. "Sure, you don't want anything else while I'm over here?" he called to his sister, "I'm not doing this again."

"No, that's fine." said Rita. "Be careful getting back." The last thing they wanted was for him to put his foot through one of the chairs or to make any kind of mark or damage that their mother would see. How would they explain that?

"Mmmn" Mohal turned and took a few moments to plan his route. Getting back was going to be harder he thought. He would have to shin over the back of the chair and the sofa from their seats. If he left any indentations they might be noticed. Taking a deep breath, like an athlete preparing for the high jump, he launched himself back towards Rita. When he got to the sofa, he took a breather and called, "Catch!" before throwing the cushion, chosen by Rita from hundreds at the Rialto market, over to her. "Careful!" Rita called back, just managing to move in time to grab the cushion with her free hand as it flew through the air. She dreaded to think what might have happened if the cushion had hit the hard, concrete floor of the storage building.

Mohal's face reappeared from behind the sofa as he straddled the back of it with his long legs and slid down to stand between Rita and the trolley.

"I hope it's what you wanted?" he said.

"Oh yes" said Rita, handing him back his phone and weighing the cushion in her hands. "Let's go." She turned to close and lock the unit's door.

"Thanks would nice" said Mohal, annoyed that his heroics had gone unrecognised.

"Of course," said Rita distractedly as they walked back together, Mohal with the trolley and Rita with the cushion, which she had placed in a large John Lewis carrier bag she had brought from home. She might be paranoid, but if anyone was watching them, she did not want them to know what they had collected.

"Could not have done it without you." she told her brother to mollify him. Mohal lifted his shoulders with pride. Rita did not notice. She was planning who to speak to next and exactly what to say.

Chapter

14

"Once did she hold the gorgeous East in fee, And was the safeguard of the West: the worth of Venice did not fall below her birth, Venice, the eldest child of Liberty."
William Wordsworth

Wednesday 28th June 2017 5pm

Rita put her head round the door of Nayan's bedroom. It was the room at the front of the house which had once been hers, just as the house, her family's home, had once been her only home and not just a place she came back to sometimes. It represented stability for her mother too, which was why she was so proud of it and the changes she had made. 10 Elm Drive was quite a step up, Rita knew, from the crowded terraced house occupied by her grandparents and their children when they had first arrived in the City in the early 1970s.

Looking into the room, Rita could not help but think back to the long hours she had spent there as a teenager, just a few years younger than Nayan was now, looking out onto the road and the houses opposite and waiting for life to begin. As she looked across the room and out of the window, the view was so familiar, as if it was burnt into her mind for ever. Even though there had been changes to the street, including the eponymous trees which had succumbed to disease when Rita was a child and been replaced with newer, disease-resistant ones, the basic details were the same. She recognised the shape of the tops of the houses, the way one home was slightly set back from another, and the colour of the brick work.

These houses, although part of an estate, had been designed, to provide homes after the Second World War, in a way that made them individual, she thought, and that made them feel homely and safe. This was so different from the rather sterile and repetitive modern housing where Meera lived, she felt. Or was it just that she had lived here all her life and it was so familiar? Maybe, in years to come, Theeran would feel as nostalgic for Chimes as she did for Elm Drive. The houses felt so permanent to her, like stalwart guardians of the street. Although the buildings had not been around for a hundred years yet, they seemed more solid to Rita than the highly decorated edifices she had seen in Venice which had an ethereal quality about them, however old they were. They were like palaces from a fantasy and it was hard to believe they were real.

This was not to say that the time she had spent in that room had been totally happy, Rita admitted to herself. Many problems had weighed on her shoulders, mainly concerning school work and friendships, as well as her annoying brothers and parents who did not understand her. The bitchiness and cliques at school had been particularly overwhelming at times. Sometimes she had sat on her bed, situated exactly where Nayan's bed was now, and wondered through tear sodden eyes and cheeks whether she would ever grow up and what it would be like. She was still wondering, Rita smiled to herself. She had come through her exams reasonably well so far, she had tried various experiences and had some scary encounters, but was she a grown up now? Would having her degree, assuming she had passed, which she hoped she had, qualify her as an adult? Did anyone ever feel they were truly grown up? she wondered. Perhaps we are all putting on an act, even the teachers and lecturers and police officers, she thought. Really, and here she could hear Athena's voice, it was not about being grown up but about continually growing, Rita thought, being prepared to change, to try to be a better person. She was not going to give up on that, she decided.

Nayan, who had been lounging on his bed gazing at his phone screen, looked up and realised his sister was standing in the doorway, in a bit of a dream. He sprang up with one bound and broke into Rita's thoughts.

"What's up, sis?" he asked, hastily closing the door to his wardrobe which was on the other side of the room, as he spoke.

"I need to speak to Mo." Rita said, registering that there had been pictures on the inside of Nayan's wardrobe which she had caught sight of briefly. Photos from magazines, perhaps, or maybe album covers. They looked like old pop stars. Had she glimpsed George Michael and Freddy Mercury? Perhaps Nayan was doing some growing up, too, she thought. Was he collecting LPs perhaps? They were back in vogue she knew. She must ask Mohal. At present, she had a more urgent task than finding out about her younger brother's musical tastes.

"Sure" Nayan replied, not asking why his sister might want to speak to his friend. He had long ago decided that Rita was plain weird. There was no point trying to understand her or what she was up to.

"Try outside Mr Cod." he suggested, standing with his back to the window, the bright afternoon light coming through the glass making him look like a silhouette. Rita squinted and nodded. She knew where that chip shop was.

Wednesday 28th June 6 pm

Evington, like Oadby, where Rita's family had lived for over twenty years, although now a suburb of Leicester, had once been a village. This was apparent from the layout and names of the streets. There was the parish church, of course, dating from the thirteenth century, with its imposing spire. Rita supposed that, in years to come, for some parts of the city the distinctive feature would be the minarets erected since the construction of several mosques and, of course, no less impressive, the Hindu temples dotted around. Beyond the church, she knew, was a road leading to Stoughton, a village to the east of Leicester, and a tree-lined lane leading to Gartree Road, which gave access to Leicester Airport in one direction and the area of Knighton, where Athena's house, Sundial, was situated, in the other.

The old village area of Evington had two roads radiating from the church, Church Road and the High Street, both of which led to Main Street, forming a triangle. A piece of recreation land lay in the area between these three streets on which a small group of teenagers were kicking a football to each other in a lacklustre fashion.

A bigger park lay across the main road, behind the library. Rita had found it when she had come here to look at a local history book. The park had been created when the Evington House Estate was bought by the City Council in 1947. Like Elm Drive, the land was used to feed the hunger for house building caused by the growth in population after the second World War. Estate land had been developed, and enough was kept back to make a large public amenity, something you did not see today, Rita thought. The estate house, dating from 1836, and built in a gracious Georgian style, was still there, serenely in the centre of a park which now boasted fine rhododendron and azalea beds, as well as many trees, some quite old and dating from the park's original use. Within the grounds, and available for public use, were six tennis courts, two bowling greens and a pitch for cricket. As in Rita's street, new elms had been planted where the original avenue of elms had succumbed to Dutch elm disease.

Rita watched as an older couple walked slowly away from the shops on Main Street. Beyond the parade of shops, roads broadened as the village had spread with collections of houses built in different phases and periods, dating from the late 19th century to the early 21st . The houses had been designed for families, with several rooms and large gardens, although the size of the gardens reduced as the building age got nearer to the present day. Many of the homes were still occupied by families, sometimes by more than one generation, while others had been converted into flats and were home to a variety of households, young and old. These were the catchment area for Mr Cod, and contained the customers who Mo would soon be feeding, when he bothered to show up.

Rita was leaning against the wall outside the chip shop. 'Mr Cod' it called itself with no nod to gender equality or fluidity. It was 5 o'clock at night and there were a surprising number of people going in and out of the shop door. There were mothers getting their family's supper, older people buying small portions for themselves, delivery men in cars and on mopeds- they did all seem to be men she noticed- arriving as if by magic but presumably in reality by the power of the internet and the phone.

Rita shifted her balance, trying not to look as if she was waiting for someone. She took out her phone, scrolled through the messages to check there was nothing new, then started to play Osmos, her latest game crush which, once she started, quickly absorbed her. At least no one would notice her while she played. What did people do in these situations before mobile phones were invented? she wondered. Pretend to smoke or read newspapers she supposed. That would look suspicious now.

Finally, a whiny kind of roar could be heard, like a tiger with laryngitis, and Mo rolled into view. He parked up, nodded at Rita, went inside to talk to the two men behind the counter, and came out again.

"Five minutes for them to bag it up" he said brusquely, not "Hello Rita" or "Sorry I'm a bit late." Mo really did seem on edge Rita thought.

"Right" she replied.

"It's a big order. Lots of burgers and fried chicken." Rita had noticed that 'Mr Cod' seemed to do a brisk trade in anything but fish.

"Might get a good tip" Mo paced nervously in the space between Rita and the shop doorway as he spoke.

"Let's sit over there?" Rita suggested pointing to a bench across the road just inside the small grassed area. Mo really needed to let go of some of that nervous energy, she was thinking. Mo glanced at the phone in his hand and looked back at the shop as he nodded and took up Rita's suggestion. It was as if he thought the delivery would disappear if he didn't watch it all the time. Seated on the bench, they were facing the chip shop. The obesity epidemic in the country was not a great mystery, Rita thought, if you watched this process. Was no one cooking at home these days? Rita felt the bench moving and realised that Mo was lifting up his knees alternately, as if he was running on the spot while sitting down. There was no chance of him putting on weight. He really could not keep still.

"I can't talk for long" Mo said, not looking at Rita but passing his eyes between his moped and the shop. "It's hand to mouth, man." Rita could see that Nayan had been right to be concerned about his friend.

"If we ordered food, could we ask that you deliver it?" Rita asked, thinking it had been ages since she and her brothers had shared a takeaway from her favourite, Happypizza Co.

"Nah. Don't work like that." Mo said, "Control. They decide who gets what job. S'posed to be rotated ain't it but it don't seem that way. They choose who they want."

"Can't you talk to them?" Rita tried to be sympathetic, even though she had a question she was burning to ask.

"Nah!" Mo snorted. "It's dog eat dog between guys like me, plus some blokes subcontract their shift."

"Is that allowed?" Rita queried.

"Oh yeh, it's all in the T&Cs. People sell on their shift to make easy money. Trouble is, a lot of the guys picking up work that way aren't exactly here legally, aren't insured etc. They can afford to do it for even less than me. It's a race to the bottom if you ask me. It's all zero hours, minimum pay and targets. I 'spect the controllers get kick-backs – you know, incentives- to favour some of the delivery guys over others. Ev'ry one's on the take these days, aren't they?" Mo seemed to take a very dim view of life, not surprisingly perhaps, Rita thought.

"Could your family help?" she suggested.

"Yeh, right" Mo dismissed the idea. "Dad divorced my mum and has another family now. Mum's on Universal Credit. It's a nightmare. Months late with payments and based on out of date information. She's up to her eyeballs in repayments to Brightlife for the furniture and stuff. I can't let her know."

"I'm sorry" Rita said just as Mo's phone rang, only it wasn't the one in his hand, it was another one, in his trouser pocket. He jumped up nervously and answered it, listening but not speaking. "OK" was all he said at the end.

"You seem to have a lot on, so I won't keep you." Rita tried not to sound curious. Mo was looking very thin these days, she thought, and after the last call his face had tightened some more. She could see that Mo was anxious and might take off at any moment.

"I wondered if you recognised any of these numbers" she asked him, slipping out from her pink satchel bag the sheet on which Simon had printed the numbers from Olga Kelenko's phone. Mo, expressing no curiosity, as if he was used to doing as he was asked, glanced at the piece of paper. He pointed to a number about half way down.

"There" he said, jabbing at it with his gloved finger. Then his other phone rang again. "Yes boss" Mo said and then he was gone, across to Mr Cod to collect and deliver his parcels of food. After that, who knows where? And for whom? Rita looked at her own phone. No time to plan what she was going to do next. She was due at the airport.

Wednesday 28th June 8pm

By 8pm Rita and Nayan were in a group of five, standing on the tarmac in the late evening sun, which was still surprisingly strong, being taken through the final preparations before their first jump. They were all eager to get going and full of nervous tension too, not wishing to show each other how apprehensive they were. They had already had a session indoors, practising the best positions to adopt when they jumped out, getting the feel of the parachute and the two chords – main and emergency- which they would have to learn to reach for behind their backs. They had seen footage of other jumps, slowed down by the instructors to emphasise certain points. Now it was time for the real thing. Each participant was paired up with an experienced skydiver with whom they would jump in tandem. Rita's partner was a strong looking woman who introduced herself as "Macarena Roberts, but you can call me Mac." Her family came to the UK from Jamaica, she told Rita, although she was born in Derby. She had served in the RAF but, as she put it, 'people like her did not get on very well there' so she was self-employed now; she sometimes acted as a bodyguard to celebrities, she said. Quite the action woman, Rita thought. Mac had a good singing voice – she belonged to the Leicester Gospel Community Choir, she informed Rita, which, she said, met in the Methodist church not far from Padma's dental surgery on Uppingham Road. To prove her vocal ability, she treated them to a rendition of 'One day I'll fly away', which Rita knew from Nicole Kidman's version in Moulin Rouge, a film that she and Priya liked to watch together. Rita approved; she thought she was in safe hands.

Small planes were buzzing in the air like giant flies. It

seemed to be a busy time for take- offs and landings. Business executives were flying in from meetings or taking planes out as a form of recreation to wind down, pretending to be in Top Gun, Rita thought. In addition to the regular flights, she saw that Nayan was being distracted by an event being run by the Leicestershire Aero Club to attract interest in aerobatics, as if Nayan needed any encouragement!

"I might get my pilot's licence one day" Nayan had said enviously when they arrived at the airport. "I want to try flying a glider next." What would their mother say to that? Rita thought.

"I don't know why you want to do these things" Padma had protested when he had first introduced the idea of skydiving at a family meal.

"It's a skill, mum" her younger son had told her "You need interesting things to put on your CV these days."

"A skill!" she had scoffed. "You'll be running away to join the circus next!" Then she had stopped and issued a stern stare to Nayan and Rita, as if to say don't even think about it.

As they entered the plane, with their fellow participants and the qualified sky divers, Rita swallowed hard. What would it feel like to do an actual jump? She would soon know.

Wednesday 28 June 2017 9.30 pm

"Yee ha!" Nayan was dancing up and down as if he had just won the lottery. "Wasn't that great?!" The jump had left him exhilarated. "Concentrate on what you need to adjust for next time" his instructor had said at the debrief. There had been lots of experts in the sky, not only those jumping with them but others to provide reassurance when the reality of being in the air for the first time caused paralysis to set in. They were positive and helpful. Encouraging those who, like Rita, had panicked at first, calming those who, like Nayan, had got over-excited. Strapped together with Mac, Rita had felt secure. The fear that went through her, just after they launched themselves into the sky, melted away as she tried to remember their training, helped by prompts from her partner. The whole jump had gone by in a blur. "Next time", thought Rita. Well, she had volunteered to go with her brother, so she had to see this through. Rita walked back to the car thoughtfully, Nayan chattering and bouncing like a spring beside her.

Chapter

15

"The hottest places in Hell are reserved for those who, in times of great moral crisis, maintain their neutrality."
Dante Alighieri

Thursday 29th June 2017 2pm

"Are you sure that's a good idea?" Priya's voice was on speakerphone as Rita searched her bedroom for the things she needed. Her task was made more difficult by the boxes and books she had brought from Leamington. They were crowded into her sleeping space until she could move out to the flat she would be sharing with Morwenna. She was also trying to be careful not to disturb the cushion which she and Mohal had rescued from the storage facility. It sat on her bed inside the John Lewis bag, and she felt it was like an unexploded bomb. The sooner she got rid of its contents the better.

"Whether it is or it isn't it's too late now!" Rita retorted. "I've set the wheels in motion."

"But you could still backout?" Priya told her, "Don't go all Mrs May on me and say you have to deliver!"

"I can't let everyone down!" Rita insisted.

"But what if something goes wrong?" Priya was insistent.

"I'll get myself out of it!" Rita was annoyingly confident, "I always do! It's like magic!"

"But you're not a magician, are you?" Priya pleaded, then she tried distracting her friend, "I was thinking about witches, as it happens, after our discussion the other day. Weren't they blamed for the plague?"

"Still have a fascination for witches, don't we? I mean,

Harry Potter and his friends are only the tip of the iceberg. Remember we used to like watching Sabrina the teenage witch?"

"Oh yes!" Rita was interested now, she sat on her bed. "And those books we read in Junior school about the worst witch!"

"Now we watch Charmed," Priya said, "And there are lots of films with witches in them."

"Somehow witches have got less scary" Rita conceded, "They are more likely to be trying to do good, or else creating comedy by getting it wrong. It's mainly women of course, Harry Potter excepted, and probably the lightness and the comedy are just another way of disguising a deep-seated fear."

"Of women you mean?" Priya was trying to follow this.

"Yes. Witches were blamed for the plague, of course," Rita was back to her study subject.

"People always look for a scapegoat!" Priya was not surprised.

"Mmmn." Rita agreed, sitting on her bed and taking an interest as Priya had hoped. "A Witch's mask is another one worn in the Venice Carnevale. There was an unprecedented intensity of witch-hunts between 1550 and 1650 in Europe, which some historians argue can be traced to the plague of 1348, which was so traumatizing. Those hunting witches took their cue from the Inquisition, which was rooting out anti-Catholics. The interrogators would try to find what they called 'plague spreaders' who would be pursued and sometimes put on trial. It was fear and ignorance that motivated the persecution, of course." Rita told her, "And history keeps on repeating itself." Rita went on, "Take the Salem witch trials in America – the ones depicted in the play The Crucible. They took their inspiration from the accusations in medieval Europe. It was the same kind of thinking."

"What about here, in this country?" Priya asked. "How

long did we go on persecuting women for being witches?"

"Oh, there were literally loads of supposed witches." Rita sighed. "One of the most infamous occasions was during the English Civil War, when a guy called Matthew Hopkins styled himself as the 'Witchfinder General' and was responsible for over 300 executions in the East of England for witchcraft between 1644 and 1646."

"There can't have been that many witches!" Priya said, horrified.

"Of course not," Rita told her, "Hopkins was getting paid for his efforts so he needed results. He relied on so-called 'confessions' of pacts with the Devil, often obtained by causing the women to be sleep-deprived. They would also tie the accused to a chair and throw her into water. If she drowned, she was innocent, if she floated, she was guilty and executed." Rita paused, thinking of Olga Kelenko, the woman she had briefly met, who had ended up dead in the water, tied to a shopping trolley. The world was not changing as fast as she would like to think.

Rita stirred herself to speak to Priya again, "In England, some of the last women to be hanged for witchcraft were from Devon. Three from Bideford were hanged in 1682 at Heavitree in Exeter." Rita told her, sighing again. "They were Temperance Lloyd, Susannah Edwards and Mary Trembles. They were accused of causing death and sickness. It was prejudice, really, but the idea of witches causing illness was very strong."

"It's barbaric" Priya said.

"And it's been going on much more recently. Helen Duncan was the last person to be convicted in England under the 1735 Witchcraft Act; this was in Portsmouth in 1944. She was basically a fraudulent medium. At least it led to the Act being repealed" Rita told her

"It is hard to credit, but a belief in witchcraft persists in some cultures today, and is used to inflict cruelty, usually on the weak, like children. They are often used as scapegoats." Rita went on.

"I know," Priya agreed. They had covered such beliefs as part of their training in safeguarding and the signs to look out for in the young and vulnerable, in particular. It was such a horrible concept that it made her shudder. "Did we have any witches in Leicester in the past?" Priya wanted to know, looking to escape from thinking about modern day horrors.

"You bet." Rita told her, "Black Annis crops up a lot in historical books about the city. She is supposed to have lived in low hills on the outskirts of the city, in a cave she carved for herself with her nails. She is supposed to have lured children there, and to have killed sheep. I suppose it was someone for the farmers to blame."

Priya interjected, "Where did those ideas come from?"

"Some think the tales might go back to a Dominican nun called Agnes Scott who was an anchorite." Rita answered.

"I know what one of those is," Priya impressed her friend, "There was one at Iffley, in that church we visited when you came to see me in Oxford, do you remember? That anchorite was called Annora. She lived in a walled-up cell next to the church."

Then Priya recalled it was while Rita was visiting her in Oxford that she had heard of her father's death. Not for the first time, she hoped she had not stirred bad memories.

But Rita was in full historical flow. "Yes. Some medieval women did attach themselves to churches for security." she acknowledged, continuing, "There is a statue of Agnes the nun in Swithland Church, apparently. She died in 1455 and reputedly lived in a cave. She wore a black habit and had a leper colony there."

"She was doing good." Priya said. "Leprosy has been so misunderstood in the past. People were scared of it. Like they were of the plague and of AIDS."

"You are right" said Rita, "So much cruelty comes from

fear and superstition." Then she continued on her theme, "There is a more tenuous connection with another witch connected to Richard."

"Our Richard?" Priya checked. The young women liked to claim Richard III as 'theirs' especially since the discovery of his bones in their city.

"Yes, you remember there was a story, and that's probably all it was, that a wise woman or witch foretold his death. As he rode on his way to Bosworth?" Rita asked her friend.

"The battle where he died" Priya put in.

"Yes. He is said to have struck his foot, or maybe a spur, on a stone. The witch or wise woman is supposed to have predicted that on his return it would be his head that hit the stone. When he was thrown over a horse after his death and his body was taken unceremoniously back to the city, his head is supposed to have hit the same stone. There is a tablet on the bridge- it is not the same bridge now, of course, it was replaced since Richard's day- which records this tale." Rita explained.

"Gosh!" Priya exclaimed, "Any more local stories?" she asked.

"There is another story involving Belvoir Castle and witches." Rita told her friend, naming a local stately home. "Francis Manners, the sixth earl of Rutland, and Master of the castle, had two women tried as witches after various members of his family and staff fell ill and some of them died. They were tried and hanged. It was all a fabrication, of course."

"It's really sad," Priya agreed.

"Hmmn. The Belvoir witches are now regarded as scapegoats and worthy of some sort of amnesty, while there have been campaigns to pardon the Bideford three. It was a shameful part of the past." Rita said angrily. "If they could, some people would prob'ly call me a witch!" she added, "I make myself such a nuisance."

"So, don't do it!" Priya was back to begging her friend, "Leave it to the police."

"I can't leave it," Rita tried to explain, "I was used by the gang and I have to try to put some of that right."

"Oh Rita, do be careful!" was all Priya could offer as the friends signed off.

When Rita had gone, Priya sat on her own bed for a while, her phone pressed to her lips, as if that would help her thoughts. After a few minutes, she sighed and turned the phone over to scroll through some numbers. "Sorry Rita" she apologised to the room, "I can't keep this to myself."

Chapter

16

"An orange gem resting on a blue glass plate: it's Venice seen from above".

Henry James

Friday 30th June 2017 6pm

They were at Leicester Airport again, to the east of Stoughton, on Gartree Road. Built in 1942 as part of the station for RAF Leicester East, when it ceased to be needed for military purposes it had become known as Stoughton Aerodrome until it acquired the designation of airport in 1974. The triangular shaped airfield mostly lay quietly among green fields, the peace disturbed sporadically by aircraft taking off, or landing, or performing tricks, like swarms of buzzing insects. Fire equipment and vehicles were prominent, Rita noticed, thinking that was a good thing; everyone was so much more aware of the risks of fire after the awful events at Grenfell tower which was still a major item of news and social media comment. Some groups were claiming that residents had been betrayed by the establishment and some were going so far as to allege a racial motive, as most of the dead were from black or minority ethnic groups. Repeatedly, their families were saying they had thought they would be safe in a country like the UK. Cladding on buildings, including the tower blocks at Leicester University, were being checked and found wanting. Something had gone seriously wrong and the fire brigade's 'stay put' policy had proved wholly inadequate in the circumstances. Rita thought no one who had seen the scenes from the fire would heed such advice in future.

The Aero Club had posters advertising their flying

lessons and Rita noticed they offered a one-hour trial. She wondered if that had caught Nayan's eye. Rita would have avoided dragging Nayan into this, but when the drop-off was mentioned she felt she had no choice. The pair were at the airport to do their second dive. This time they would be jumping alone, which was even more daunting although there would be instructors in the sky to make sure they remembered what to do. Rita had been hoping to see Mac again. She had given her such confidence last time. But she was not there and the only instructor on the ground, who was talking them through the dive to come, was Lek, a Polish guy who had jumped with one of the other participants last time. While he spoke, Rita looked around anxiously for the other experienced instructors who would help them.

As on the last occasion, the closer the time came for the jump, the more Rita wondered why she was doing this. Her mouth was dry and under her layers of clothes she was sweating. She tried to recall how wonderful it had been to land at the end of the first jump. Focus on that she thought. Of course, there were other reasons for her nervousness. As well as looking out for her favourite instructor, she was scanning the airfield for strangers, people who looked like they shouldn't be there. But everything looked pretty much like it had the previous time. She did some stretches, insofar as it was possible in her jumping gear, and tried some deep breathing to keep herself calm.

Nayan, by contrast, was getting hyped up. "Vimana" he said out of nowhere.

"What?" Rita asked, confused.

"In Hindi it means aircraft." he told her, "Like the flying palace, which is a really common sculpture on temples, you must have seen one. Amazing that the ancients foresaw air travel!"

"I guess" Rita agreed reluctantly, recalling that the pictures she had seen were of buildings several storeys high whirling through the sky, so a little unlikely.

"I'll go check the plane is ready" their instructor said and disappeared. Rita and Nayan waited, keeping their knees flexed in their blue jump suits and their bodies supple as they had been taught. Both were wearing sturdy trainers on their feet and on their heads they had the leather hats with which they had been supplied. Rita's face was tight with apprehension. Nayan was grinning with the same feeling. Funny how it affected people differently, she was thinking, when Nayan broke into her thoughts.

"Hey, where's our instructor gone?" he said, looking first at the plane and then around the airfield, which seemed fairly deserted compared to when they had last jumped.

Nayan had barely spoken when brother and sister both felt a hard object pressing into the back of their necks between their hats and the collar of their jump suits.

"Do not move. Do not turn around. If you do, I guarantee you will not walk again" Voices whispered menacingly into their ears. Rita felt her legs go to jelly. This was all her fault she thought. She had put Nayan in danger.

"You, come with me" she heard and, to her horror, Nayan was taken away. He and his escort were just dark figures in the periphery of her vision. She daren't turn her head to see more.

"Leave him alone" she managed to cry out in a voice made squeaky by not taking a proper breath first.

The hard object was pressed close to her spine.

"Shut up!" said the deep voice of a man, some foot and a half taller than Rita, about the height of those tall tennis players Rita had seen on television, she thought irrelevantly. She and Priya had talked idly about going to see some tennis, maybe at Queens or even Wimbledon she found herself thinking. She squeezed her eyes shut, then opened them again. She needed to focus, concentrate on what was happening, remember details in case she lived to tell anyone about this.

"This way" the man grunted and pushed her towards the plane.

"What? No!" At first Rita tried to resist, too shocked at what was being proposed and the possible implications.

"No choice" her abductor said. He didn't seem to have a wide vocabulary, and was that an Eastern European accent, a bit like Olga's, that she detected? Where was Nayan, what was going to happen? Rita almost tripped as her knees started to give way. The man lifted her off the ground with one arm and put her down, on her back, on the floor of the hold of the plane. Rita started to struggle, feeling like an upside-down beetle, flailing her arms and legs to get them to work together so she could sit up. The hold door closed. Her kidnapper was gone. Rita's heart was beating very fast now, and her breath was coming in short bursts. I must keep calm she thought as she tried to stand. In the cramped hold it wasn't easy to get her balance.

A large figure came out of the shadows and loomed over her.

"It is better to be sitting down when the plane takes off" a man's voice said. His words were muffled by the balaclava which covered his mouth. The stranger pushed Rita on the shoulders to make her do as he said. Rita stared into the gloom. She had been so busy with what was happening to her that she had failed to notice the plane engine was throbbing. Now they were taxiing for take-off.

"No" she said in panic, trying to stand again, although it was difficult as the plane lurched, gathering speed.

"Sit down" said the voice in the shadows even more firmly, and she saw a large knife moving in his gloved hand. He meant what he said.

All at once, the plane started rocking from side to side, sending them both staggering, their bodies clashing, and Rita found herself sitting on the floor. She felt the plane bumping more quickly along the runway and then the bumping abruptly stopped, her stomach left her body, and she knew they were airborne.

* * *

"Hand me the drugs." the figure in the gloom said, holding out one hand while still clutching the knife in a threatening manner with the other.

"Can't I stand up now?" Rita pleaded, thinking it would be easier to do what he wanted if she was on her feet.

"Get on with it!" he hissed back impatiently.

Rita stood up unsteadily, using the straps in the hold to help her balance. She reached to unclip the black triangular pack fastened to her chest. It was a relief to be honest, the bag was quite heavy. She held it out. The stranger stepped forward, crouching and snatched at the bag with his black gloved hand.

"Got it" he spoke into a radio fastened to his shoulder and stepped towards her as, to her horror, the hold doors opened. Air whistled into the small space and the temperature suddenly dropped, but that was not the main thing that Rita noticed. Mesmerised, she could see the earth yawning below, an immense carpet of greens, browns and yellows with wisps of white cloud interrupting the view.

"Enjoy the flight" the stranger said as he took Rita in a judo grappling hold, lifted her off her feet and, before she could take another breath, propelled her out of the gaping doors.

Chapter

17

"When I went to Venice, I discovered that my dream had become- incredibly, but quite simply- my address."
Marcel Proust

Friday 30th June 2017 6.45pm

Mohal was racing across the runway, heedless of the dangers of any planes that might be landing, of the officials in high visibility jackets and gilets who were waving him out of the way, and of the police car which was bearing down on him. Not naturally athletic, he had never run so fast in his life. He stopped to get his bearings, then ran on, past a hangar and into a small area of woodland at the side of the airfield. He was looking frantically from left to right, his breath coming in short bursts, like a panting dog. The top of his head felt prickly, whether from the sweat he was generating or the fear that was gathering from his stomach to his chest, he could not tell.

He had just known this would go wrong. His sister was too much of a risk-taker. He had been thinking that ever since Priya had rung him, after Rita had told her what the plan was and sworn her to secrecy. Priya knew she couldn't keep the information to herself. Someone in Rita's family needed to know, someone who would know what to do. Mohal had listened, his jaw hanging open, as Priya explained what Rita had told her. When the call had ended, Mohal had been transfixed for a moment. What to do? Then he had decided. Rita would just have to put up with it. He had scrolled through to find Dr Sharma's number.

Now Mohal's eyes were shifting around, desperately

scanning the grass and the trees beyond the airstrip, willing himself to find his brother and shutting his mind to what might have happened to his sister.

"At last!" he gasped. "Oh mate. You ok?" he addressed the forlorn figure of his younger brother, his hands tied behind his back, tape over his mouth. Nayan was propped up against a tree, looking like a guy on bonfire night.

"I'm ok" Nayan whispered after his brother tore off the tape somewhat painfully.

Mohal took a bottle of water from his back pack, unscrewed the top and handed it over. "I saw the whole thing" he told Nayan. "They gave me a pair of binoculars when I was sitting in the unmarked police car near the runway. Oh man, I was so scared for you. The feds were not expecting firearms." Mohal's shock was making him garrulous.

"Where's Rita?" Nayan asked, in between grateful gulps of the water. To his shame, his hands were shaking so much that some of the water splashed onto his blue jump suit. He wanted to look brave in front of his older brother, but he didn't feel it.

"She went.." but, before Mohal could tell Nayan that their sister was airborne, the brothers heard a noise.

Behind them, they could hear the crunch of steps in the undergrowth and then the panting breath of two figures who appeared through the foliage. They were wearing dark shirts over black jeans. Nayan, who had risen from his seated position and had been leaning against the tree, stumbled back in alarm, his eyes wide with fear.

Mohal caught his arm. "It's ok" he reassured him, "They are police."

Friday 30th June 2017 7pm

Dr Sharma and Constable Malek were speeding through the Leicestershire countryside, keeping a close eye on the dot that was beeping on the screen on the dashboard of the police car. When he had heard the plan from a worried Mohal, Dr Sharma had insisted on accompanying the operation. He felt he owed it to Padma. As they cut along country roads and tried to guess where the dot was going, both men had one question echoing in their heads, was Rita still alive? The NCA had put trackers on the drugs and on Rita. The fact that the dots were not together any more could mean only one thing. Rita was not with the drugs and, since the undercover team had seen the plane take off with her in it, she was probably not in the plane.

The winking dot had stopped moving. It was fairly clear they had reached their destination. In a field, about 500 metres from the road, could be seen some material billowing in the faint breeze.

"Wait there!" the officer told Dr Sharma, holding out his hand in admonition as he opened his car door and climbed out.

Dr Sharma pretended not to hear, and followed him over to a metal gate which it was easier to climb over than try to open as it was padlocked on a metal chain. Dr Sharma jumped down the other side about 30 seconds after PC Malek and began to stumble over the uneven ground which had once held a crop – some sort of broccoli maybe? Bits of green plant kept impeding his progress but, on the other hand, he was pleased to see the field was used for crops and not animals. He had no wish to tangle with an irate cow or bull.

Surprisingly, he was gaining on the Constable, who was giving his HQ a running commentary, literally, as they sped as best they could to the middle of the field. It must be the dread making me move quickly, Dr Sharma thought, I'll pay for this later. They arrived at the site almost simultaneously. Dr Sharma took one look and bent over, his hands on his thighs, waiting for his breathing to return to normal. Both men stared at the sight. The parachute bobbed up and down every so often. Rita was not there.

As if to be sure, the Constable took out his baton and poked at the fabric and the harness, trying not to disturb it too much but checking there was nothing or, God forbid, no one, underneath the tent which the parachute had now formed. As he performed this task, both men noticed two things. There were splashes of red noticeable against the black of the harness -possibly blood? - and parts of the harness had been slashed. Both men were thinking, 'Where was Rita? Had she ever been attached to the parachute? When and how had she become detached?'. The two anxious men stared around the field, looking for clues from the ground and the bits left over from the crops. There was nothing.

The officer's radio crackled and the voice of his controlling officer could be heard asking him to explain his status. "OK. Got that" Control said when the Constable had explained." Back-up is on its way to examine the scene" then, before the two of them could conduct a more thorough search of the field and its surroundings, Control spoke again, this time in urgent tones. "Suspect spotted on the Ashby Road driving away in a red Ford Focus Registration DT15 KXH. You are the nearest. I am authorising you to carry out a pursuit." The pair, who had barely recovered from running towards the parachute site, jogged back to the patrol car as quickly as they could.

"He might be dangerous" the officer said to Dr Sharma as he turned the car round sharply and sped back the way they had come, then took a left turn which was quickly followed by a right. The lanes were narrow here, barely the width of a car, with passing places every few hundred meters. The sensation, Dr Sharma felt, must be similar to the feeling you get when on a car rally. He felt he should be helping the Constable but there was nothing he could do. He had not understood what Control had said about the location of the red car and where to intercept it. He was not familiar with this area of the countryside. They were on the other side of the field now. Dr Sharma could see the mushroom shaped parachute basking in the evening sun. But all their attention was now on the red Ford Focus which was now just ahead of them, taking the corners of the country road at reckless speeds. Constable Malek did the same. Dr Sharma clung on to his car seat with one hand and put his other hand on the dash board to steady himself.

Without warning, the Focus braked. Constable Malek braked too and swerved in the direction of a gravelled passing place which had appeared to their left. In this way, he was able to make sure the cars did not make contact full-on. His patrol car hit the other car a glancing blow. The police car went left and came to a halt at the end of the passing place, the Ford Focus shot over to the right and collided with a gate a little further down on the opposite side of the road.

"Stay put" the Constable ordered, as he undid his seat belt and jumped out of the car. Again, he was ignored. Dr Sharma, his legs shaking, climbed out and, since the police car had its bonnet in a hedge, crept slowly towards the back of the vehicle. It was then that a black figure emerged, limping, from the Ford Focus.

"F*** off coppers!" he yelled and then Dr Sharma heard a cracking sound and suddenly the police officer was lying on the ground in the middle of the narrow lane, between the two cars. Dr Sharma was uncertain what to do. Should he get back in the car and try to radio their predicament? But he had no idea how the communication system worked. The Constable, still prone, had a radio on him which he might be able to use if he could reach it. His first instinct, in any case, was to help the stricken officer, although that would put him literally in the firing line.

His moment of indecision did not last long. As he emerged from behind the rear of the patrol car there was another crack and he felt a searing pain in his left leg just below the knee. Dr Sharma found himself sliding down the back of the car and onto the lane. Now all three men were lying on the ground, the gunman having collapsed after he fired the second shot, whatever injuries he had sustained in the crash apparently having overwhelmed him. After he had keeled over, he had tried to crawl towards the police car, but ran out of energy, like a toy with run-down batteries.

Dr Sharma was sweating with the pain in his leg and breathing in short gasps. He could hear the police officer's radio calling for information. "What is your status? Come in Constable Malek." Then, more pleadingly, "Ravi, are you OK? What's happening?" Dr Sharma tried to stand, to limp, to drag himself to the injured PC and his radio, but the pain was too great, and he passed out.

Friday 30th June 2017 7.30pm

When Dr Sharma next opened his eyes – he had no idea how long he had been unconscious- he thought at first he was dreaming. Everything was very blurred as he struggled to get his eyes in focus. Perhaps he had bumped his head as he fell? Maybe he had lost one of his contact lenses? They were bi-focal. He needed them for close work and for distance; too much studying, his late wife would have said.

It seemed to him that a dark figure wearing a black peaked cap was bending over the gunman, checking for signs of life, and putting him in the recovery position. Dr Sharma could not see another vehicle in the vicinity, let alone a police car or an ambulance. Where had this person come from? Had they been in the crashed Ford Focus? Was this another of the gang? he thought. Would it be better for him if he pretended to be dead? Dr Sharma did not need to worry. As the figure straightened up, he lost consciousness again.

Opening his eyes slowly once more, Dr Sharma realised

that he had been helped into the patrol car; he found himself propped up on the back seat on the passenger side. His seat belt had been fastened for him. The lifeless body of Constable Malek was being pushed onto the back seat next to him. Then a dark figure got behind the wheel.

With a loud snapping sound, all the doors were locked by the driver, the figure he had seen wearing a cap, the engine turned, and the car put into reverse. A hoarse voice spoke from the driver's seat.

"Call the police. Tell them we're going to hospital."

Dr Sharma fumbled in his pocket for his phone, and fainted for the third time.

Friday 30th June 2017 7.40pm

"Stolen patrol car" was the first thing DCI Jamie Bridge's driver heard. The Chief Inspector was on his way back from a high-level conference on internet fraud at a hotel near Castle Donnington, not far from East Midlands Airport. For once, he had the luxury of an unmarked car and a driver, which meant he could catch up with some work. He had his lap top open and his papers were spread out across the back seat. "Always working" his ex-partner would have said, "You need to take a break sometimes, Jamie." The differences in their work ethic had been a major factor in their break-up, he reflected, as he looked through his emails.

The grey BMW was another 30 minutes from Leicestershire Police HQ in Enderby, his next destination for a briefing meeting on the woman who had been found in the canal. Apparently, there had been some developments involving the NCA. DCI Bridge sighed. He did not want to be late for the briefing, but the driver had been forced to take the A6 to avoid congestion on the M1 caused by an overturned lorry which was blocking two southbound lanes.

"Sorry Sir, call from Control, we're the nearest vehicle."

his driver called over her shoulder, putting on the emergency lights and siren and speeding up, taking a turning to the left onto a B road and then left again onto a country lane. At the hump back bridge, before he could collect them up, DCI Bridge's papers fell from the seat to the floor. There was no time to retrieve them. He managed to close his lap top at least. He put it back in its bag and leaned forward as far as his seat belt would allow to talk to the driver.

"Where are we going?" he asked "What's happening?"

"A patrol car has been stolen on a lane near Shepshed. The circumstances aren't clear. The car was chasing a suspect, so it's possible the suspect is driving." she told him.

"I see" said Jamie Bridge, "What about the officer involved?"

"No information, Sir" he was told "The back-up team are just arriving at the scene where the patrol car's whereabouts were last reported, so we may hear more soon."

The driver and the DCI stared at the road ahead. Above them, they could hear the whirr of blades; the helicopter had been called in to track the patrol car from the air, using the number on its roof. Whoever was driving would know they could not get away.

"The patrol car has turned onto the A511 towards Leicester. Let me know when you get eyes on." Control relayed to them the information they were getting from the air.

Reaching the junction with the A511, the driver made a fast right turn in the direction indicated, and soon the patrol car could be seen ahead of them.

"You are authorised to pursue. Suspect may be armed" the voice on the radio said in reply to this information from DCI Bridge's car. "There may be one or more hostages among any passengers. Observe but take no risks."

Jamie Bridge's driver put her foot down.

"Let's hope there are no pedestrians." she said grimly.

"We have to do our job as best we can." the DCI replied,

realising they were both thinking of a recent incident with a neighbouring police force where a passer-by had been knocked down and killed by a patrol car responding to an emergency. You could not get it right all the time, Jamie Bridge was thinking.

They were gaining on the patrol car as it entered the dual carriageway, heading towards the city centre. Where could the vehicle be going? How did the driver expect to escape? In all probability he was panicking, making it up as he went along, the DCI was thinking. This made the situation very unpredictable. They had reached a built-up area; there were houses lining both sides of the road. If the gunman opened fire it would carry a huge risk to the public, but they could not wait for the armed police unit to get to them.

"Going alongside." the driver said, talking simultaneously to Jamie Bridge and Control. "Will report status" and she sped up.

They were almost level with the patrol car now. It was making no effort to outstrip them. Perhaps the driver of the marked police car was injured? Ahead of them, the DCI and his driver were aware, other officers were endeavouring to empty the road, to make it as safe as possible in the circumstances and to set up a road block, using a 'stinger' if necessary, to stop the car if the driver refused to do so. The operation would be very popular with people trying to get home after the hold-up on the motorway DCI Bridge thought.

Now it was possible to see inside the patrol car. There were two passengers on the back seat, one person, the driver, in the front. DCI Jamie Bridge reported this to Control while his driver concentrated on keeping the cars in parallel and checking the road ahead was clear for both vehicles. "Two men in the back, one sitting, one lying down" he reported, "Both IC4. The one sitting looks about thirty with short dark hair. Clean shaven. No clear visual on the one lying down. The driver…" he began as they moved forward a little more, his driver ready to drop back if a gun was pointed at them, "The driver…" but he could not finish the sentence for astonishment.

The driver had been wearing a black peaked cap. As it was removed, brown curly hair cascaded down.

"Rita Patel !" Jamie Bridge exclaimed to the surprise of his driver who watched as Rita took a hand from the steering wheel and raised it in a wave of acknowledgment.

Chapter

18

"If I were not King of France, I would choose to be a citizen of Venice."

Henry III

Friday 30th June 2017 7.50 pm

Control was speaking again, "We understand from a call from a gentleman in the car, who seems to be a dentist, that they are going to Glenfield Hospital. Can you confirm from your observations that that seems credible?"

"Affirmative" Jamie Bridge said, reporting that the body lying on the back seat seemed to be in a police uniform, and the man sitting upright next to him was talking on a mobile phone. There were no weapons in sight.

"Can you provide an escort please." Control requested. "All road blocks have been removed. The helicopter is still airborne and will follow to the hospital." The officer in charge of the operation was taking no chances. Despite their observations, DCI Bridge realised that one of the passengers, or someone they could not see, could have the others under duress.

* * *

Although having no A&E Department, a volunteer team of medical staff at the hospital were on hand as the patrol car entered its grounds and drove to the main entrance, closely followed by DCI Bridge's unmarked grey BMW car. Everyone else, staff and patients, had been moved to the back of the building. Ambulances had been put on stand-by to ferry any injured to other hospitals which specialised in trauma should that be necessary, and the fire brigade had sent a tender too, just to cover all the possibilities. The operational commander felt short of solid intelligence about what was going on.

The control centre was getting the observations of DCI Bridge and his driver simultaneously with reports from the scene of the crash with the red Ford Focus, where a male IC1 had been found on the ground in the recovery position. He had stomach and head wounds consistent with involvement in a high-speed shunt into a metal fence. It was indeed against such a fence that the car, which an NPR search showed to be stolen, had come to rest, its bonnet buckled. There were also reports coming through from an airfield near East Midlands Airport, where the plane containing the drugs had landed. Several unidentified males had been arrested and a quantity of cocaine seized. It was unclear whether they had caught all the gang involved, and exactly how the dentist and Rita Patel fitted into all of this had yet to be established.

Dr Sharma, weak from the wound in his leg, was stunned to see armed police officers open the doors of the patrol car simultaneously, declaring 'clear' in quick succession. Then they stepped back for paramedics to kneel to assess the wounded passengers. Dr Sharma was helped into a wheelchair, the police officer was carefully moved onto a trolley. Both were quickly taken inside, the paramedics shouting out injuries and vital signs to the doctors who met them at the door.

DCI Jamie Bridge himself, a pair of evidence gloves on his hands, opened the driver's door wider, having ascertained for himself there was no additional person hiding in the footwell on the passenger side. Rita was slumped against the steering wheel, exhausted by her efforts.

He crouched down. "Well done Rita" he said softly, "I might have known!"

Rita turned her head to look at him without lifting it from the wheel.

"You'd better get the armed police back." she said in a cracked dry voice he barely recognised, "There's a gun in my belt."

149

Chapter

19

"I did not write half of what I saw, for I knew I would not be believed."

Marco Polo on his deathbed

Friday 30th June 2017 7pm

For a second or two after being thrown from the plane, Rita had experienced nothing. The shock was total. Among the scenarios she had tried to imagine, this had not been one of them. In her mind the outcome had not been like this, propelled into the air miles above the ground, all on her own. After the immediate numbness, lots of experiences and thoughts came rushing at once, like a film on fast forward or a crowded press conference when everyone asks questions at the same time. She could hear the gentle hum of the plane as it drifted away into the distance, and the rushing of the air as it passed her or, rather, as she passed it. She could feel the blood pumping in her ears as if they would burst as her heart went into red alert. She could not see which way up she was. Either she was spinning, or the earth below her was, or both.

Get a grip she told herself, at last remembering some of the training they had received. She checked the altimeter on her wrist. Having a solid fact like how far above ground she was might help. She saw it was time to pull on her chute. Rita did her best to take up the position they had been shown, sort of like she was swimming on her stomach, and felt behind her harness for the chord. She was vaguely aware of a pain in her right side as she did so, and the harness did not feel as tight as she would have liked. Perhaps something had come loose when she was propelled from the hold?

Rita pulled. Rita waited. She stopped breathing. She found herself fighting to keep her body in the right position, as the instructors had shown them. She never expected she would be doing this alone. Then there was a whooshing sound! The canopy had opened and was pulling Rita upwards. It was going to be all right, she thought, instinctively clinging with her right arm onto the harness as if she might slip out of it otherwise. She just needed to hold her nerve.

To keep calm, to the extent that was possible, as she drifted downwards, Rita decided to conduct a quick mental inspection of herself. Her head did not feel too bad, considering she had banged it as she was half helped, half thrown into the hold of the plane. Her back and legs would probably be bruised, but they didn't feel useable now. She would need to flex her knees and bend her body on impact. The only real pain she had was coming from her side where the man's knife, pointing at her threateningly, must have come into contact with her when the plane jolted. It must have been quite a lurch as the knife had penetrated the layers of her sweat shirt and jump suit to get through to her skin. The cut might be deep, but she couldn't worry about that now. I need to concentrate on landing, she thought, trying to visualise all that they had been told in their training.

"I can do this. I can do this." she repeated to herself.

Rita checked her altimeter again, looked down to see that the ground was still far away, and tried to put recent events in order in her mind. Once she had the drugs from inside her mother's cushion, which she had realised the gang and the police must have missed, and had made the connection between a phone number in Olga Kelenko's contacts and one that kept giving 'special delivery' orders to Mo, it had been her idea, which she explained in a phone call to DC McKenzie, to call the drug dealers and arrange a drop off. The police were hoping that at least some of the smuggling gang would be caught. Rita was hoping there might be evidence linking them with Olga's watery death.

When she made contact, with DC Fryer listening in, she was surprised to be asked when she was jumping next and to be told to go to a particular hangar at the aerodrome when all the pre-flight preparations were done. The NCA were in charge of surveillance. They had put trackers on the package and on Rita. With the police and her older brother, who had been alerted to the arrangements by Priya, in whom Rita had confided, keeping watch, what could possibly go wrong? She had not expected to be forced onto the plane at gunpoint and she certainly hadn't expected that Nayan would be threatened. She hoped he was OK. Her mum would never forgive her if he came to harm.

I can do this, she repeated once more. The ground was getting closer now, as verified by the altimeter. It was up to the NCA to intercept the aeroplane, using the tracker on the drugs package. Her own tracker had been in her watch, which she had worn on her right wrist to leave room for the altimeter on her left arm. The watch strap had broken when she was pushed down by the man in the plane. In the gloom of the hold, she had pressed the watch into her harness. She hoped the watch was still travelling with her. She could not look for it. She had to keep as still as possible and prepare herself for contact with the ground.

Those involved might not be the top guys, Detective Sergeant McKenzie had told her. But the police would use the operation to gain some intelligence and at least disrupt the gang's activities. It is risky, he had warned her. She did not need to be told. Look what had happened to Olga Kelenko. How close had she got to identifying the members of the criminal gang who were operating in the Midlands, the ones who must have intercepted the packages which Matteo so cheerfully and callously sent Rita home with? They must have felt threatened if they found it necessary to torture and kill an unarmed woman. What quantity of drugs or amount of money was worth doing that? she pondered. Once involved in these criminal activities, it seemed that any sense of proportion disappeared. As the officers who had interviewed her in Leicester had said, each person in the chain feels under pressure from someone above. Nothing was beyond them, they were so desperate. It explained why they used school children, often those excluded from school in fact, to deliver drugs and messages. They picked on weaknesses and everyone was expendable.

Rita could start to see where she was coming down. It was fields criss-crossed with country lanes, like a giant noughts and crosses grid. There was an area of woodland which it would be wise to avoid, if she could. At the edges of the fields were fences and hedges. A hedge might just break her fall and would be easier to get out of than a tree she reasoned. It would be better still if she could land in the middle of one of the green or brown patches. Recalling what the instructor, Lek, had said – what had happened to him by the way? was he in league with the drug traffickers or had he been taken away too? she puzzled- Rita did her best to hold on to the harness and guide herself to safety. It was a hard job as, all of a sudden, the ground was coming towards her at a tremendous speed.

Thump! Rita's plans to land gracefully had gone awry. Her poor bruised backside had taken another hit. Lying flat on the ground, she sat up carefully. Her arms and legs felt OK, if a bit shaky, her chest was tight as if all the air had been expelled from it. Her left side was sore. She took some deep, rather painful, breaths, then stood and slipped out of the harness which separated from her quite easily. She had no idea where she was, and no means to contact anyone, since her assailant had taken her phone. There was no telling how much danger she was still in. She could spend precious time searching through the parachute for the tracker, so the NCA could find her, but she felt very conspicuous in the middle of this field and thought it best to get to the edge and make her way to one of the roads she had seen from above.

What if a member of the gang was in the area? No need to be paranoid she had told herself. Reaching a hedge in the corner of the field, she unzipped her blue jumpsuit and stepped out of it, stowing it inside the hedge together with her leather hat. Underneath the jump suit she had been wearing a black sweatshirt and tracksuit bottoms. From her waist pack she took a black peeked cap and pulled it on. Then she headed for the corner of the next field, inching her way towards a road.

Rita had no plan as to what to do - flagging down a car looked an attractive option, but what if it was driven by someone in the gang? Could she take that risk? Breathless, she fought her way across the field where some sort of green vegetable had been grown and harvested, leaving green debris behind in the hard, brown soil. Rita tried to weigh up her options. There were no phone boxes these days and she could see no sign of a building where there might be a phone. It was just empty fields as far as her eyes could see.

Maybe she should wait for a vehicle that looked safe. An AA or supermarket delivery van might turn up, she thought, surely it was unlikely that they would be infiltrated? They would be able to contact their headquarters and raise the alarm, wouldn't they? She just had to keep out of sight until the right vehicle came along. Rita looked at the sky, where the sun was still shining. She had perhaps another 30 minutes before it started to set, she thought, and the light lasted for a long time on these June evenings, didn't it? She could find a place to lie in wait until a vehicle came by that looked safe to approach.

Rita was less than a hundred meters away when a red car flashed by on the road, closely followed by a white police car. Too closely, clearly, as there was a horrible screeching sound and a loud bang. Fuelled by adrenalin, and forgetting her plan, Rita broke cover and ran to see what had happened.

Chapter

20

Robert Benchley

Monday 17th July 2017 11 am

The TV weather forecaster, who Rita consulted while she dressed, promised that the day of her graduation would be dry and warm, the temperatures would be average for the time of year, and the sky would be overcast. The humidity was reported to be low, the pollen count was high. Putting her head out of the window of her room in Brunswick Street – they were due to give the keys back to the landlord the following week - the air felt clear, not like the claggy atmosphere of Venice, she thought. The weather prospects suited her. The academic gown over her black dress with the blue flowers would be warm enough, and she preferred to be without a jacket, she had enough to worry about with her bag and mortar board. She had not realised the headgear was necessary until she had visited the hire shop.

"Oh yes!" the assistant had told her, "Essential for the photographs."

"Well, why does it have that strange name?" she wanted to know, still not sure about the object she was being offered. "I was told it was thought to resemble the board that masons use to hold mortar- the cement that goes between bricks- but I gather the original idea came from a sort of hat called a biretta which used to be worn by scholarly clergy centuries ago." the assistant had explained with a shrug of her shoulders as if to say, 'Don't blame me!'.

Rita had sighed. She liked history, but she did not

particularly want to have to enact it. She preferred to leave that to the historian on the TV, Lucy Worsley, who was always keen to get into costume. Surely someone could have come up with a better outfit for a graduation ceremony by now? Tradition was all very well, but academia was like religion, she mused, slow to move with the times. Still, if Priya could do her exams while wearing her gown – a shorter, less cumbersome, version than the one Rita had been given, to be fair- surely she could wear it just for her graduation? Rita had seen pictures of Priya after her last exam, covered in silly string after the traditional Oxford 'trashing'. At least they did not have that practice at Warwick. Thinking that her mother would be proud of her, she had thanked the assistant for her help, gathered up the hat, folded the gown over her arm, and left the shop.

Like most of her female friends, for her graduation Rita was wearing silver sandals on her feet, another reason to be grateful for the reasonably fine day they were promised. It was the only item that really showed beneath the gown which, when she looked at herself in the mirror as she prepared to leave, was all encompassing and not at all flattering. From Rita's observation, for the men, wearing the gown over their suits and ties, lent them a sort of dignity, but for the women it looked more like they were being disguised or covered up, and the hat was hard to wear with some hairstyles. It was pretty clear which gender the costume had been designed for, in Rita's view.

Thinking ahead to the ceremony, her mother and Priya would be arriving at the Rootes Building, where it would be taking place, in the Chancellor's Suite, in an hour or so. Rita had said she would meet up with her fellow graduates on the campus in the Costa coffee outlet next to the hall. There was a family meal to look forward in the evening. They had booked a table at Kayal, one her favourite restaurants in Leamington, and a variety of friends and relations were coming. But, before she could go to the coffee shop to join the others, Rita had one more task to perform.

Rita walked into the Registrar's office or, rather, the anteroom where the Registrar's secretary sat. "You can't come in here today we are very busy.." Siggy began to say before she looked up from the piles of paper and printed spread sheets she had organised to ensure the day went smoothly for all concerned. It was like arranging an Oscar ceremony, she thought, and no one wanted a 'Moonlight' moment when the wrong announcement was made. All the details had been double-checked. Nothing must spoil this special day for each student, if that could be avoided.

"Oh" she said when she saw the graduate before her was Rita, her gown over her arm, the skirt of the black and blue dress swinging with the motion she had generated when she climbed the stairs to the office. Across her body she wore her black bag with the elephant motif. Rita took something out from under the black gown. Siggy stood up and backed away against her chair as if afraid that Rita might have a weapon. Her reaction told Rita a lot about the sort of people that Siggy had been dealing with. She was not waving a gun or a knife at the administrative assistant. It was a book, a copy of The Divine Comedy, which Rita dropped noisily on Siggy's desk, not worrying if she disturbed the paperwork.

"I believe all debts have to be discharged before graduation" Rita said, "I don't have any library books or fines, but I do have this. I can't give you the one you gave me as it is in the hands of the police. I do not know if there is enough evidence to prosecute you, they are waiting to hear from the CPS, but I wanted you to know that I know what you did. You set me up. You have probably set up others before me. I have nothing but contempt for you!" Rita's voice was calm and measured, but very determined.

"I.. I.." Siggy began to say, but Rita had turned on her silver heels and walked out of the door. She need not think about that woman again.

Monday 17th July 2017 8pm

Padma sat at the head of the table in the restaurant in Regent Street, Leamington, at Rita's insistence. The staff had been very friendly and forbearing as Rita's friends and family members had arrived in different groups and everyone began talking before they even sat down. Now, seated at last, they were exchanging pictures and videos from the graduation. Rita actually liked the photo of her in her gown, after all, with Padma in her sky-blue suit on one side of her, and Priya in a yellow dress on the other. Their faces were lit with happiness. Dr Sharma- Mahir as he had insisted she call him when she had visited him in hospital - had made them laugh just before he took the picture with his phone. For once, Rita was pleased with her hair. Her former housemate, Daz, who had four sisters, had pinned it up for her with surprising expertise. It had stayed in place for the whole ceremony and even threatened to keep in place for the celebratory meal. In the pictures, her black dress with the blue pattern on it looked very elegant under the gown, she thought. The mortar board she just held in her hand, it did not look good on her, although there were pictures circulating of her wearing it and holding her degree certificate. No doubt one of those would be gracing her mother's living room soon, alongside a similar shot of Mohal. Like the empty fourth plinth in Trafalgar Square, a third space awaited Nayan; "No pressure then", he had been heard to say.

Other pictures were circulating too. Rita had footage on her phone from the memorial service which had taken place the day before for Olga Kelenko. Her former boyfriend, Ryan, had organised it at the school and anyone who knew her was invited to attend. Rita was sorry not to be able to go, but she had too much to do to prepare for her graduation ceremony and empty the house on Brunswick Street. DS McKenzie and DC Fryer had been there, apparently, as well as officers from the local police force. People had wanted to give something in her memory, Ryan had told her, so he had set up bursaries in her name to provide financial support for pupils at the school from poorer backgrounds who wanted to go to university. Rita thought Olga would have approved. Every single person she could see round the table now had contributed to the new Kelenko Foundation.

Padma glowed with pride as she looked down the table at the people who were gathered to celebrate her daughter's success. Rita had achieved a 2:1 in her degree and had a place on a law conversion course, so that one day she would be a solicitor, a qualified lawyer. It was all that she and her husband had hoped for. Rita was sitting to her mother's left, and Priya was next to Rita. The young women had their heads together, looking at scenes from the graduation which had been posted on line. Opposite Rita, and on her right, Padma had placed Dr Sharma. Her thinking was that if the young people got engrossed in taking pictures of their food or looking at their apps, which they had a habit of doing, she would have someone sensible to talk to. She missed Rita's father, Jahi, so much on these occasions. How he would have loved to see this!

Detective Chief Inspector Bridge, sitting beside Dr Sharma, was talking across the table to Rita. She had not thought he would be able to come to the meal when her mother suggested inviting him, but it turned out that there was a police conference at a hotel near the M69/M6 junction which he was attending, so it all fitted in.

"Very good of you to invite me, Rita" Jamie Bridge was smiling, "No firearms on you this time, I hope?"

Rita smiled, turned her open hands towards him and lifted up her arms, covered in the sleeves of the turquoise dress she had changed into for the evening, to show she had no weapons on her. As she did so, the cut she had sustained in her side gave her a small twinge of pain, a little reminder of her recent adventures. She was not going to let that affect her.

"Don't worry" she laughed.

"I think the police officer might have died if you had not arrived when you did and got him to hospital." Mahir Sharma joined in. "I was in and out of consciousness," he explained to the Chief Inspector, "Which is why it took me so long to ring the police. I was not in a fit state to do much for the officer." he added regretfully, shaking his head.

"Constable Malek will make a full recovery" DCI Bridge confirmed, "Although it will be a while before he is back to full duties. He had a lot of stitches. He is grateful to you Rita."

"He was very brave, from what I heard." Rita said, then turned to speak to Priya again, but she was engrossed in a conversation with her brother Mohal, who Padma had placed on Priya's other side. What were they planning now? Rita wondered. It was her birthday soon. Perhaps they had a surprise in mind? Across the table, she saw that Nayan was now deep in discussion with Jamie Bridge, their hands waving animatedly in the air as they demonstrated their points. Nayan's visit to the police station, arranged by the DCI, had gone well, Rita gathered. Perhaps if he didn't kill himself flying, he would make the police force one day, she thought, they needed enthusiastic recruits to combat the ever-growing threat of gangs and organised crime.

DC McKenzie had told her that the gunman from the red Ford Focus had survived the crash thanks to the air bag although, perhaps because he had not been wearing the seat belt, he was in a bad way when they found him, having suffered concussion, some broken ribs, internal bleeding and a ruptured spleen. His DNA matched the DNA found on the shopping trolley in which Olga Kelenko's body had been moved and half submerged. It seemed that the trolley had perhaps not sunk as far as the criminals may have intended.

Other members of the gang had been apprehended when the plane landed and the drugs from the cushion were recovered. As the police had hoped, a supply line had been disrupted. Some of those responsible would be tried and, if all went well, convicted. But, as DC Dominic Fryer had told Rita, it was an uphill task. The Brexit situation did not present a happy prospect, either, she had learned from him. While talks were continuing with the EU, it was looking like UK police forces might lose vital intelligence links with their European counterparts. If so, this would make identifying members of international gangs, not to mention policing the Irish border, which was getting increasingly contentious, that bit harder.

The trattoria, like many legitimate businesses, had been used for money laundering, she had learnt, as Olga Kelenko had suspected and had died for her suspicions. There was a lot of illicit money swilling round in the system now, Jamie Bridge had confided in her, making it impossible, despite money laundering regulations, to differentiate from finances garnered lawfully. It was even said that, in the financial crash in 2007/8 when property prices crashed, it was drug money rather than quantitative easing which kept the banks afloat.

"Will you have to take the stand again?" Nayan was asking his sister. "You know, will the police need you to testify?"

Rita shook her head and shivered a little. The last time she had been a witness in court had not been a happy experience. "No, no, no, I do hope not." she said.

Mohal, to keep things light and not spoil his sister's day, decided to tease his younger brother, "We say 'go into the witness box' in this country," he said, "You watch too many American programmes, bro! You'll be talking about trash cans and closets next!"

"Yeh, yeh!" Nayan challenged back and the pair began a mock fight, throwing their napkins at each other, until halted by their mother's reproving look.

Further down the table from Nayan, their cousin Shona,

wearing a sliver sheathe dress, her sleek hair tied in a knot on top of her head, seemed to be chatting happily to Sammi and across from her Shreya, in a gold version of the dress and wearing her hair down and full of waves, was talking to Daz. Rita had said nothing to their parents about seeing them in Veenos and, later, outside on the pavement. She hoped that was the right call. The twins needed to grow up in their own way she told herself. They would be going to the same uni in the autumn, both having been given unconditional offers, she gathered, a growing trend for universities anxious to increase their student numbers.

Their mother, Jaina, sitting beside Shreya and opposite her husband, Bandhu, was beaming with pride at her daughters' confidence. She worked as a secretary at the girls' school and had seen at first hand the quality of the education that she and Bandhu had paid for. In Jaina's view, it was not that her sister's children had done badly as a result of their state education, it was just that they lacked, well she would never say it to Padma, a certain 'polish' that private schools provided. She had confided to Padma before the meal, in Rita's hearing, that their education had given her girls social confidence. You don't know how confident they are Rita had thought.

Rita had also resolved to say nothing to Priya about having seen her brother- in- law in an inebriated state in the company of the twins. It was not her business, she decided. It was between Meera and Jai what they did. But she would be listening out carefully for any signs of a rift, and she would put Priya straight if she started to blame her sister without having all the facts. Hopefully, whatever the problem was Jai would get it out of his system before the new baby was born. There were four lives involved here, Rita did not want to intervene and risk making things worse.

Doctor Mahir Sharma was smiling at Rita across the table.

"It is good to see you happy again" he said. "I was so worried about you after the police interview."

"I know," Rita admitted, leaning across the table to hear his deep voice better above the chatter of everyone else in the restaurant. He was recovering well after being shot. The bullet had gone right through his leg apparently, which Priya said was better than if it had lodged inside, and had missed his knee cap by a few centimetres, so, although he had lost a lot of blood at the time, the injury was not as complicated as it might have been. His leg was still sore and he walked with a slight limp. Tonight, he was looking very smart in a black suit with a nehru collar over a charcoal shirt, his short dark hair looked like it had had the attention of good barber. Since the accident he had grown a neat beard which he wore trimmed close to his face and which somehow made him look younger. He was the epitome of style, Rita thought, while her two brothers were wearing their usual open neck shirts, although they had put on chinos rather than jeans to honour the occasion.

"Perhaps I will be able to see more of you if you are going to continue your studies in Leicester?" Mahir Sharma was saying.

"Yes" said Rita "I expect so," adding, after a pause, "That would be nice." Then she smiled at Dr Sharma before turning her attention to her blackcurrant sorbet. He sat back and smiled too, before picking up his fork to tackle his vegan cheesecake.

Everything is changing, Rita thought. She would miss seeing her uni friends and walking the streets of Leamington and Warwick. But the people stay basically the same, she told herself, and they had vowed to keep in touch. She was glad to be coming back to her home town to work and study, although she wondered what sharing with Morwenna would be like.

As if reading her mind, her mother took Rita's hand and spoke, "Well done Rita, your father would have been so proud."

Rita grinned back at her.

"No more adventures now." Padma squeezed her daughter's hand as if to extract a promise, "You'll have to settle down. You'll need to work to pay your part of the rent for Morwenna's flat while you do your law conversion course. You won't have time."

"I know you worry mum," Rita said softly, and then, turning to face her younger brother over the table, "And I'm sorry I led you into danger, Nayan. I really never thought…"

"Well it's time you did think, Rita!" her mother put in sharply.

Dr Mahir Sharma and Rita's brothers looked at each other and smiled. All three rolled their eyes simultaneously. Like that was ever going to happen.

Rita Patel returns in
Body in the Cathedral

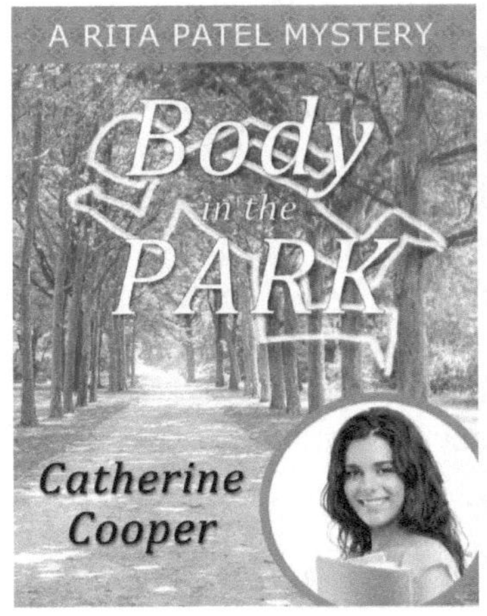

ISBN: 978-1-910779-68-2

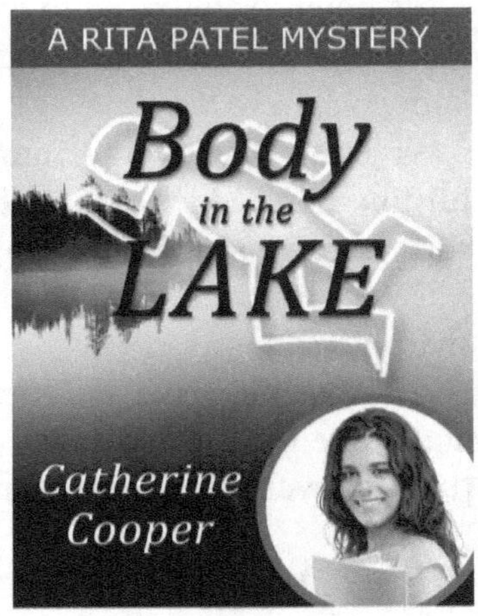

ISBN: 978-1-910779-69-9

ISBN: 978-1-910779-70-5

ISBN: 978-1-910779-71-2

ISBN: 978-1-910779-72-9

ISBN: 978-1-910779-73-6

ISBN: 978-1-910779-74-3

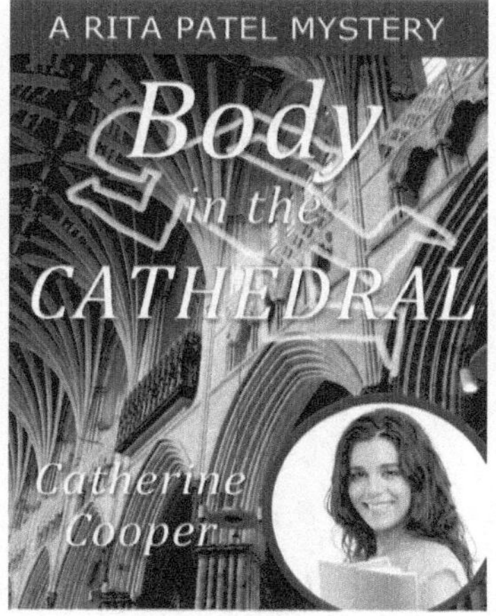

ISBN: 978-1-910779-75-0